PENNSYLVANIA PASSION

ROMANCE ACROSS STATE LINES

DEBBIE WHITE

© 2019 by Debbie White

All rights reserved. Except as permitted under the U.S. Copyright Act of 1976, no part of this publication may be produced, distributed or transmitted in any form or by any means, or stored in a database or retrieval system without the prior written permission of the publisher.

This is a work of fiction. Names, characters, organizations, places, events, and incidents are either products of the author's imagination or are used factiously. Any resemblance to actual persons, living or dead, or actual events is purely coincidental.

Editing by Kerry Genova, writersresourceinc.com

and

Leo Bricker Grammatical Eye®

Cover Design by Larry White

Debbie White Books

Summerville, South Carolina

Maddy Pryor left in a hurry. She packed two suitcases, tossed in Fluffy's dog bed and toys, and off they went in search of adventure. Actually, she was running. Running as far away as she could from her creep of a boyfriend. The old adage, the straw that broke the camel's back? Well, it just happened. Ryan took out his anger on her for the last time. The straw, when he kicked Fluffy. She looked over at the sleeping pile of white fluff and watched as he snored softly. "Who wouldn't love this?" she mumbled under her breath.

It was true Ryan didn't like dogs, but he didn't care for Maddy all that much either. He cursed at her continuously, made her feel less than human, and when she challenged him on his verbal attacks, he always managed to turn the tables and make it her fault. She thought she could "change" him. You can't change someone who thinks women are beneath you and spews verbal offensive attacks on you like it was normal. Who does that? And, why did she put up with it for so long? Acceptance. But what she couldn't understand is how and why she felt like this. She had two loving parents who worshipped her and had believed in her. But the bad boy syndrome was real for Maddy, and she'd fallen for it a couple of times.

When she confided in her mom that things weren't going so well with him, she suggested a change. Maddy was sure she didn't mean as in location, but it called to her one night after a particularly stormy fight with Ryan and him kicking Fluffy. Enough was enough.

They weren't driving far. Maddy wanted to be close to her friends and family in Philadelphia. She'd traveled the state before and recalled the sleepy little villages in Lancaster County. She headed there. Even if he were to look for her, he'd probably not think Amish country. But who was she kidding? He'd never look for her.

Thank goodness she had a mobile business. She'd started it from the ground up. Going to people's houses, washing and grooming their dogs. She'd saved up enough money to purchase a van equipped with a sink and a grooming table. Taking her business on wheels with her meant she could set up shop anywhere. The question was, was there a need for her services in Lancaster County?

She arrived within a couple of hours. Getting out of Philly traffic was the worst. When she arrived over the county line of Lancaster, she found a place to pull off and rethink her plans. She didn't have any plans per se; she flew by the seat of her pants most days. This wasn't much different except she also told her boyfriend of three years to go fly a kite, and not in those sweet terms.

"Let's see, Fluffy. According to Google, there's a real estate office two point two miles ahead. Let's go see what sort of things are for rent around here. But first, I'm going to stop and get some lunch and walk you."

MADDY LEASHED up Fluffy and headed inside. *I hope they are pet-friendly.*

"Hi," Maddy said to the lady sitting behind the desk. "I just came into town. Wondered what the availability was regarding rentals?"

The lady's gaze lowered to Fluffy.

"It's kind of warm out. I don't like to leave him in a hot car."

The lady cleared her throat. "What are you looking

for exactly?" She pushed her dark-rimmed glasses up on her face and crossed her arms.

This lady reminded Maddy of the old school librarian back in high school. "A one bedroom is all I need."

She turned her attention to her computer, not saying a word about what she was doing, but just clicking her mouse and studying the screen. Maddy figured it out shortly. She must be searching for listings. After about three or four minutes, she spoke.

"The only thing I have available is a loft over a barn."

"Are they pet-friendly?"

"I don't know why not. It's a dairy farm. John Cooper's dairy farm," she said, speaking in monotone, driving Maddy crazy.

"What's the rent on it?" Getting her to give details was like pulling teeth. "Terms of the lease," she added.

"Let's see," she said. "Rent is eight hundred dollars a month and includes utilities. It's month to month, and he requires the first month's rent in advance."

"That's doable. Can I get the address?"

Mrs. I Don't Have Much Of A Personality made a phone call to Mr. Cooper and informed him of their upcoming visit. Maddy followed her directions and arrived at the dairy farm within ten minutes. She drove through the open gates and noticed the wrought iron detail with the cow and the big sign saying, "Cooper Dairy Farm." She pulled up the long gravel drive and parked. A modest, white clapboard house with a large wraparound porch was to her right. Off in the distance, a huge barn and several fenced-in grazing pastures. She could smell the agriculture and farm animals as soon as she stepped outside her van. Looking at the barn, she wondered if that was where the loft was and could she handle sleeping above the manure smell that was so prevalent. She shook her head. Maybe this wasn't a good idea.

Just then, a man came out of the house, wiping his hands on a towel. "You must be Maddy," he yelled.

"Yes. Maddy Pryor, and this is my faithful companion Fluffy."

"Mobile Pet Grooming," he said, nodding toward the graphics on the side of her white van.

Maddy smiled and motioned toward the van. "Yes, I've been grooming pets for over three years. Do you have any?"

All of a sudden, three dogs came around from the back, barking and wagging tails. They sniffed Fluffy under her tail, making her jump. When they realized she was not the enemy, they stood back.

"That's Marcus," he said, motioning at the large-headed shepherd. "Over there is Scruffy. He's a Jack

Russell, and over there," he said, pointing to the black-and-white dog, "is Hazel, the border collie."

"I guess no farm can be complete without dogs." Maddy petted Marcus.

"I have one more, but she's inside. She was my—anyway, she's inside."

"Can I take a peek at the loft?"

"Sure, follow me."

He led her to a smaller barn that was behind the big one. She couldn't see it from where she'd parked.

"It's more like a tool shed. We keep the tractors in there and some miscellaneous items."

"Okay. I was worried for a minute it was over the cows." She laughed.

"I can't guarantee you won't smell anything, but it won't be direct."

When he smiled, his eyes crinkled up at the corners. He spoke coolly and softly. There was no hurry in his voice, and Maddy liked that. Made her feel comfortable, like a well-worn hoodie on a cool fall day.

They climbed the wooden stairs up to a small landing. He quickly opened the door.

The loft was one large room with a bed and dresser on one side, and a couch and chair on the other with a short wall separating the two halves. Along the back wall, a kitchen that consisted of a couple of cabinets, a sink, a mini apartment-sized stove and refrigerator.

"The bathroom is over there." He pointed to the far corner.

She glanced inside. An insignificant corner shower, a pedestal sink, and the toilet took up every inch of space. It was tiny but contained the essential elements.

"Closet?" She whirled around, looking.

"No, just this." He walked over near the bed and lifted a cover, exposing a metal rack suitable for clothes and a shoe rack on the bottom.

"That would work. I don't have a lot of clothes anyway. The rent is eight hundred dollars a month and includes all utilities. Is that correct?" Maddy locked eyes with John.

"Yes. Does that sound reasonable?"

"Sure. I'll take it."

"Great. I'll call Mrs. Calhoun and let her know you're taking it. You'll need to fill out the lease paperwork with her and leave her a check. She handles all of the leasing requirements for me."

"Okay, good enough. When can I move in?"

"Today."

Maddy and Fluffy headed back over to the real estate office. She wanted to get her paperwork filled out and any money to Mrs. Calhoun before someone else took it right out from under her. It was a perfect place to live. Quiet…except for the mooing, fresh air…except when the wind kicked up…and a nice landlord. *One out of three ain't bad.*

She quickly filled out the one-page lease agreement, handed over a check for the first month's rent, and grabbed the keys before someone told her it was all a mistake.

Maddy made a fast stop at the local market and purchased some essential items like toothpaste, toilet paper, soap, and shampoo. She tossed in some ramen, plain potato chips, and a bag of red whip licorice, her one big weakness. Well, two if you count the chips. She had dog food, and it was a good thing because the market didn't carry Fluffy's brand. She'd either have to order it online and have it delivered or seek out a pet store.

When she arrived at the farm, a horse and buggy were pulled up alongside the main house, and John and an Amish gentleman were talking. He flipped up his hand in a wave. She parked the van in an open space and got out.

"Maddy Pryor, this is Ezra. A friend of mine."

"Hi, Ezra," she said as she opened the side door of her van and retrieved Fluffy and the bags of groceries.

"Ezra and I go way back. He's done some work for

me. In fact, he was instrumental in the construction of the loft you're going to call home." John dug his hands in his jean pockets and flashed her a grin.

"That's nice. You did a great job. I'll be very comfortable there." She tugged Fluffy's leash. "Come on, boy."

"Have a good evening. If you need anything, holler."

She stopped and turned around. "There is one thing. Is it okay to park closer to the loft?"

"Oh, sure. Just drive around the back side. There's a gravel area where you can park. I'm sorry. I should have mentioned that."

She juggled the two bags and Fluffy's leash, wishing she'd just put all of it and the dog back in the van and started over.

Before she could even do that, John was right next to her, taking the bags out of her hand. "Let's put this back into your van. You can drive around back and park. No sense walking that far and lugging this up the stairs to the loft."

He'd read her mind. How cool was that?

She unloaded the few groceries she purchased, left Fluffy sleeping on the floor, and went back down to the van to get the rest of their things. John was just headed back to the main house when he noticed her.

"Just getting the rest of my things."

"Can I help you?"

"Well, if you don't mind." She opened the back of her van.

He reached in and grabbed both suitcases. She pulled out Fluffy's bed and a few odds and ends. "Thanks, I really appreciate it," she said.

"I hope you enjoy your new place," he said, looking around.

"I know I will. It's perfect for us. I'm going to start spreading the word about my mobile grooming service, so if you want to do the same, that would be fantastic."

"I don't know how many people have dogs that require grooming, but I'm sure if not in this town, maybe the next one over."

"I'm willing to drive up to twenty miles or so."

He slowly backed out of the loft and started to take the stairs back down. She felt like their conversation ended suddenly and wasn't sure what to say to make it feel complete.

"I'd be happy to give your dogs a bath…for free."

"Those old farm dogs?" He chuckled. "I spray them down occasionally with the hose. Now little Sheba, that's a different story. I usually take the clippers to her myself, but that really wasn't my forte. Sarah used to do that."

"Sheba? Sarah?"

"If you have a minute someday, stop by the house. I'll introduce you to Sheba."

"I'll do that. Oh. Hey, John?"

"Yep."

"I don't suppose the loft has internet." She shrugged and flashed a wide grin.

"No, but if you want it, just call the cable guy, and he should be able to hook it up. I don't have much need for those things."

"Those things? You mean like searching the internet, or having programming ability with your tablet?"

"Right. I don't even have a television."

"Seriously? Wow. Well, I can't live without being connected to the world."

John cocked his head. "There's a big world out there to be fully connected to without some electronic contraption. But I get up at the crack of dawn, and on most nights fall to sleep with a book pressed against my chest. No time for television."

"Books are great. But I read them on my tablet," she said.

"I had a television before. It's not that I'm opposed to it, but so many times it can take your life over, and you forget to enjoy the little things in life like fresh air, long walks, and working with your hands."

"True. Kids now days can't function without their

iPad or cell phone. I hear you. But it's important for my business to stay connected. It's how I advertise my services too."

"Hey, far be it from me to tell you how to run your business. Take care. Let me know if you need anything."

She closed the door behind him. Her gaze dropped to Fluffy with his paws stretched out, blinking his lashes and tapping his tail on the floor rapidly. Looking at her watch, Maddy realized it was dinnertime for them both.

After a bowl of ramen and applesauce for dessert, Maddy took a long shower. Realizing she'd not packed any towels, she had to dry off with a couple of tee shirts. Unrolling her sleeping bag, she laid it on top of the mattress. Tomorrow she'd go into town and buy a set of sheets, a pillow and blanket, and some towels.

Without any internet, her laptop and phone were pretty much useless, so she got out paper and pen and began to jot down ideas for her grooming business. Her stash of savings wouldn't last forever.

She must have fallen asleep at some point but woke up to Fluffy barking. Rubbing her eyes, she slipped out of her sleeping bag, sitting on the edge of the bed. "What's wrong, Fluffy?"

Fluffy began dancing around and going in circles. That meant one thing. He had to go potty.

Maddy pulled a long sweater over her camisole top

and lacy shorts she slept in and slipped on her flip-flops. She leashed up Fluffy and descended the stairs. Downstairs was eerily creepy and dark. This wouldn't work. She'd need a light of some sort. Put flashlight on the shopping list, Maddy, she said to herself. They gingerly took the stairs and made their way through the barn and outside. Thankfully, the grounds were lit up like a Christmas tree farm. Fluffy did his business, and just when she began to turn and go back inside, she heard a man's whisper.

Her head jerked around. Narrowing her eyes to the shadow, she could see the outline of a body. A man's body. Was that John?

"John, is that you?"

"Yes. I hope I didn't frighten you."

She watched as he came out of the darkness, her heart still beating fast from being startled. She jerked her sweater tighter so as not to reveal too much skin, although her legs were exposed.

"I was out checking the area. I do it before I head to bed. Just to make sure the cattle are all good. We have coyotes and things that run wild out here, even a bear or two, so you should be mindful of that."

"I need more light in the barn. It was very difficult to see."

"I can install a motion light. Would that help?"

"That would be awesome. Otherwise, I was going to buy a flashlight. I'll try to get Fluffy to do his business before dark."

"I'll stand here until you get safely inside."

"Thanks," she said softly.

"Good night," he said.

The control of his voice relaxed her and steadied her heartbeat. A landlord and a gentleman. How lucky could she get?

CHAPTER 2

*H*er first priority was to get internet in the loft. She drove into town in search of the cable company. Fluffy went everywhere with Maddy and perched in the front seat; he had a front-row view to the outside. There wasn't a whole lot to see. One farm after another dotted the countryside, along with the occasional horse-drawn buggy. She slowed way down when she passed them, waving as she did.

After the long, drawn-out process of getting internet and securing a date for installation, she headed a little further north. It was a beautiful day. The sun was so bright that even her sunglasses couldn't keep Maddy's eyes from squinting. Fluffy finally curled up and went to sleep.

She came across a roadside sign showing the way to homemade baked goods. One thing Maddy knew for sure, the Amish women could bake. She followed the signs and pulled into a quaint barn-style building with a full front porch. She wouldn't take a chance that Fluffy could overheat inside the van, so she rousted him awake, hooked his leash to his collar, and helped him down to the ground.

She cautiously opened the heavy door and stepped inside. Immediately, the wonderful aromas of sweet baked goods wafted all around her senses. Sugar, cinnamon, vanilla, yeast, all the good things that went into baked goods stirred up her hunger pangs even more.

"Good day," a woman said, wearing a burgundy dress with long sleeves, a white apron, and a white bonnet tied under her chin.

"Hello," Maddy said. "It smells so yummy in here." Her gaze floated to the counter where loaves of specialty breads wrapped in cellophane were stacked neatly in rows. Down below the counter, pies. Lots of pies.

"How can I help you?"

Maddy loved the accent used by the woman, the German dialect, or Dutch as some referred to it, was so pronounced.

She read the labels identifying the goods. "I'll take a banana bread loaf, and an apple pie, please."

She had no idea how on earth she'd eat it all, but she couldn't resist the urge to at least try. She paid the nice woman, bidding her a good day, and Fluffy and she trotted out to the van, carrying their sweet treats.

When Maddy passed the small newspaper office, she quickly pulled in. It was a last-minute thought, but some people still took the newspaper, especially in the country where not everyone followed the news electronically.

The clerk behind the counter was also friendly. Except for the agent at the real estate office, everyone in Lancaster was full of smiles.

"I'd like to place an ad."

The clerk helped her fill out the request. "That will be ten dollars. It will run Friday, Saturday, and Sunday."

"Okay. Can I extend the ad?"

"Sure. We're not open on the weekend, though."

"I see. Well, let me go ahead and extend it now through the week. I really need to drum up business for my mobile grooming."

"I have another option for you."

Maddy tilted her head.

"The local radio station can run an advertisement for you. I think they charge one hundred dollars, but it reaches two villages and beyond."

"Thank you…Carl," Maddy said, reading his name tag.

He quoted her the new price for the week-long paper ad. She paid him and headed off to find the radio station. It wouldn't be hard. Carl said to look for the radio frequency tower.

The road that led to the station was long and dusty. She drove slowly, but her tires kicked up the dirt and rocks anyway. She came to a stop in front of the small, primitive-looking building. The cement structure was painted a drab yellow, with two small windows, one on each side of the door, peeling paint, and on the stoop, a once-thriving houseplant begged to be mercifully put out of its misery. She knocked then opened the door, tugging at Fluffy's leash, persuading him to stop sniffing the dead plant.

A man with headphones was sitting behind a plate glass window, mashing buttons, and pulling levers. She stood for a minute then tapped on the glass. He glanced over to her and grinned, holding up a finger.

He came out from behind the glass. "Yes?"

"I just came from the newspaper office, and Carl told me I might be able to get you to advertise something for me."

"What did you have in mind?"

Maddy informed him of her grooming business, Scrub-A-Dub Dog.

"Sure, I can do that. I don't know how profitable a mobile dog grooming service will be here in the country, but you never know."

"It's ideal for elderly people who can't drive, busy people who can't find time to take their dogs in, that sort of thing," she said, trying to sell her business to the radioman.

He held up a hand. "You don't have to convince me." He laughed. "I'll do my best." He went over to the counter and jotted down a few lines. "How about this?" He presented her with the paper.

Her eyes followed the lines. When she finished, she let out a burst of snickers. "You just came up with that? You're good."

"I thought it was catchy. Scrub-A-Dub Dog mobile grooming service. Call Maddy today. She'll *pawsitively* have your dog smelling sweet."

"How much do I owe you?"

"You're new in town, right?"

"Yes."

"For newbies, fifty dollars."

She dug in her purse that was slung across her shoulder and retrieved some bills. She counted them out before handing them over. "Thank you."

"No problem. I hope you get a lot of calls."

Feeling confident she'd done everything she could to get the word out about Scrub-A-Dub, she headed back to the dairy farm.

Pulling into the farm, she drove around back. She could see about half a dozen or so men dressed in over-alls, some with hats, working in the fields. Parked along the edge of the fields, lined up one after the other were two black buggies with horses nearby grazing. She wondered if John was any of the men. She twisted to the right. Extending her arm, she grabbed a cloth bag to load up her baked goodies. Heading up to the loft with Fluffy, all Maddy had on her mind was a slice of something sweet followed by a cup of coffee

In the city, it took forever to get service people to come and do things. So, to her delight, when she checked her cell phone and saw she had Wi-Fi, she shrieked. Maybe living in the country had more benefits than just clean air.

She powered up her tablet to make sure it was up and running. She'd felt so out of the loop even if it was for only twenty-four hours. Online now with all her electronic devices, Maddy scanned stations on the clock radio left in the loft to see if she could find the call letters, CRKN. She stumbled upon the familiar voice as he introduced the upcoming songs. She listened to a few tunes, and as she began to turn the dial, she heard it.

"Hey, all you animal lovers out there. Are you tired of driving all over town to get your dog groomed? I have just the answer for you. Call Maddy at 820-456-3450 of Scrub-A-Dub Dog mobile grooming service. She'll *pawsitively* get Rover smelling sweet again."

Maddy leaned back, a wide smile plastered all over her face. Now, she'd wait for all the calls to come in and start scheduling. She leaped up and moved toward her compact kitchen. "This calls for a celebration."

SHE DIDN'T HAVE to wait long. Later that day, she received four calls from senior citizens living in a nearby community. The following day, she got a few calls from single people who barely had time to think, let alone get their dogs groomed. Before the week's end, she had a full month of services scheduled. Proud of her achievement and getting the word out about her grooming service, Maddy was able to rest. With one less thing to worry about, like where her next meal would come from or the money to pay John for rent, and after a full day of getting the van ready, exploring her new surroundings and devouring her baked goods, she fell asleep. With her clothes on and Fluffy at the foot of her bed, both of them snoring softly. Maybe just from exhaustion, maybe from the overload of carbs. Either way, nothing but a wrecking ball the size of the Grand Canyon could have woken them.

CHAPTER 3

Fluffy came along with her on all her grooming jobs. The dogs seemed to sense him being there as more of a calming presence than a nuisance. They sniffed and wagged tails, and then, of course, the treat bag always came out. Maddy talked to her clients as she bathed them, clipped their nails, and yes, even brushed their teeth. It amazed her how many clients didn't know the importance of clean teeth and gums in their fur babies.

She met some nice people at all her stops too. There was Mr. Pringle, who made her laugh whenever she said his name. It reminded her of the chips in the can. Mrs. Carlson with Pippi, the poodle with apricot-colored fur. Ken, the young lawyer who lived in one of the villages and provided a lot of free work to the

Amish in exchange for fruits, vegetables, dairy, and smoked meats. But one of her favorite customers was a pair of old ladies who bickered nonstop but seemed to be joined at the hip. Sisters from another mister, forming a true bond even in their elderly years with not one, not two, but three chihuahuas. Li'l Bit, Peeps, and Chaz were darling little dogs. She'd just finished bathing them. While Li'l Bit and Peeps stayed in the comfy kennel with a heat lamp, she blew Chaz dry and rotated the other dogs out for the blower. Their tiny bodies shook continuously until they were warm and dry.

After she finished those three, she and Fluffy headed home. She pulled into the long drive of the dairy farm. John was in a rocking chair out front on the porch, his three big dogs lay nearby, sniffing the air. A small black poodle sat in his lap.

Brushing off the fur from her grooming smock, she tried to look a little less frumpy. For who, she asked herself as she straightened her hair. Fluffy jumped down and started to head over to the porch.

"Fluffy," Maddy called as she ran after him.

"I'm sorry about the intruder," she said, making light of Fluffy's escape.

"No worries. I think it's better the dogs get to know one another anyway."

They watched as everyone got acquainted like dogs do, sniffing in private territory.

"Who's that?" Maddy asked, pointing to the black bundle he held.

"This is Sheba."

"She's darling," Maddy said as she rubbed Sheba's head.

"She belonged to my—" A sigh danced on his lips. "My wife."

Maddy's expression slackened. Compressing her lips, she paused, not sure what to say next. He was married. Did that really change anything? It shouldn't. He was just her landlord.

"Wife?" she asked.

"She passed away about a year ago. Sheba was hers."

Now feeling like a chump who totally got it wrong, she wondered if her pinched look gave it away. "I'm so sorry, John. I didn't know." She glanced over to Sheba.

"Cancer."

Maddy nodded, not sure what to say.

"We'd only been married for two years. One year of married bliss and the other fighting the worst disease possible."

Maddy hung her head, hiding her emotions.

"Anyway, didn't mean to be such a bummer," John said, turning slightly away from her.

Avoiding an awkward situation, she couldn't let him go off feeling as if he'd rained on her parade.

"Why don't you come up for dinner tonight. Bring Sheba. Fluffy and she can hang out while I try not to poison you." She hooted at her dry humor. "I don't really know how to cook. If it doesn't come in a can or box…"

"Why don't you come over here instead. I have homemade spaghetti sauce simmering on the stove now."

"Homemade sauce? Wow, I'm impressed."

"When you live off of the land, you learn to make a lot of things. It's a long way to the supermarket."

She knew that was right. She'd been stopping at the little countryside market, picking up a few things and seeing the cost.

"I'll be over after I get my shower." She looked down at her smock and blew the fur off.

"Great. See you then."

SHE HAD few clothes with her. She just didn't dress up. In her line of business, it was jeans and a tee shirt covered up by one of her grooming smocks. She settled on a pair of slim-fitting jeans and a lavender top. It seemed to complement her red hair and green eyes. Or so she'd been told. She slipped on a pair of sandals, pulled her hair back into a ponytail, inserted some silver hoops, and stood back and looked at herself in the mirror. She reached for her makeup bag that contained only a light foundation, mascara, and lipstick and decided a little wouldn't hurt. Lastly, she spritzed on a light floral cologne.

They stood on the porch after tapping on his front door. When he yelled for them to come in, she slowly opened the door, stepping inside. "Hello. It's us," she said, closing the door behind her and Fluffy.

"I'm in the kitchen. Come on back."

She glanced around as she followed the sound of his voice. A dimly lit living room and dining room, a long hall, and soft yellow lights with white cabinets coming into view let her know she was getting close to the kitchen. The smell of tomatoes and garlic also convinced her she was on the right path.

She moved through the threshold into the kitchen. Adjacent to the kitchen, there was a small dining area and family room with a brick fireplace on one wall. "Something smells divine."

"Thank you," he said, tipping his head. "Please." He pointed to the stools lined up along the counter. "Have a seat. I'm just putting the finishing touches on our dinner."

She sat and looked around the room. Modestly decorated, the home definitely lacked a feminine touch. There were no pictures on the walls, no knickknacks, and except for one small picture—of who she assumed was Sarah—sitting on a side table near a well-worn recliner, the place was void of anything decorative.

Fluffy found Sheba, and after exchanging a few nose rubs, Sheba shared her big soft bed with him.

"They hit it off well. You don't let the big dogs in the house?"

"I do, but at night. Just before we get ready to go to bed. They are out protecting my land from intruders."

She watched as he drained the pasta. "Can I help with anything?"

"Maybe just pour us a glass of wine. The glasses are over there," he said, pointing with his shoulder.

She jumped up from her stool and circled the counter. She poured the wine.

Pulling on oven mitts, John retrieved a foil packet. "Garlic bread," he said, tossing it on the counter.

"I'm hungry. I really worked up an appetite today." She moved her hand in a circle over her stomach.

"Grab a plate. We're going to eat casual. Sauce is here, bread is there. Oh, I almost forgot. The salad." He whizzed around and opened the refrigerator.

"Man, you do know your way around the kitchen."

They sat at the counter. She took her original place, and he sat on the end facing her. The first few moments were taken with her devouring the food. When she came up for air, she began to thank him for inviting her.

"You're welcome. I'm happy for the company. It gets lonely here at night."

She swallowed a piece of the garlic bread down with a sip of her wine.

"I get lonely sometimes too. But for a different reason than you," she said, her words fading.

"Loneliness is loneliness." He twirled pasta around his fork.

"My parents live in Philadelphia," she said.

"Big-city folks," he replied.

"They live on the outskirts, but yes, a big city."

"Why did you leave?"

"I left because I needed a fresh start. I'd just broken up with my boyfriend of three years. He was verbally abusive. I put up with it for so long. He'd been faking a lot of things with me, but when I found out he hated dogs, that was the final straw for me. I can't be with someone who hates dogs. I just can't."

"How'd you find that out. Did he tell you?" John swirled the wine in his glass.

"I saw him kick Fluffy. At first, I wasn't sure I saw

what I thought, but then I saw him yank his tail and make him cry."

"I'm not a psychologist, but it sounds like he didn't like a lot of things. He has anger issues, period."

"I about lost it then. I packed my things fast, and we were out of there. My parents let us hang out with them for a while until I figured things out. But I was used to living on my own. It's hard for a thirty-year-old to move back in with their parents. Not to mention, bring a dog."

"Fresh starts are good. Just moving forward is good." His voice trailed off.

Sensing the conversation was going south, Maddy tried to lighten the mood. "I'm so happy to have found your loft for rent. It's the perfect place for Fluffy and me. My mobile grooming business has taken off just as I'd hoped. Do you know Ethel and Bertha?"

John chuckled. "Who doesn't know Ethel and Bertha. Sisters from another father."

They both laughed so hard and loud, the dogs began to bark.

Maddy pushed back her plate and moaned. "That was so good. Thank you again. It was nice to have a home-cooked meal. Ramen can get old."

"Ramen. Is that what you were going to poison me with?" The corners of his eyes crinkled.

"I was going to open a bag of salad too." She pouted.

"Did you save room for dessert?" He reached for her plate and slid it on top of his.

"Dessert. Oh my. Let me guess, homemade brownies, maybe chocolate chip cookies."

"Apple strudel."

"You made apple strudel?"

He shook his head fervidly. "I didn't make it. But the Amish women in town make the best desserts. So, it is homemade, just not by me."

"I bought some of their goodies. I ate a whole loaf of their banana bread. I know what you mean."

"Coffee?"

Over slices of strudel and freshly brewed coffee, John and Maddy talked into the night. It was so late when she left his place, Hazel, Marcus and Scruffy, his dogs, were sitting on the porch waiting to get let inside.

He opened the door and let them trot inside. "Let me walk you guys home." He pulled the door closed.

"That's not necessary. It's just around the corner."

Shrugging, he said, "Bears and coyotes."

"Oh. That's right. Sure. That would be awesome." Her smile faded quickly. She leaned over and picked up Fluffy. She didn't want to take any chances of some wild animal carrying off her baby.

In the darkness of the night, a light chill drifted. In the distance, she could hear howling. As they came closer to the garden, a pair of yellow eyes stared back at her. She let out a scream. Fluffy barked, and John threw his arm across her as if he were saving her from some beast.

"What. What is it?" His tone rose in pitch as he glanced around.

"Eyes. Over there. Must be a coyote," she said, her voice full of alarm.

Just then, a cat ran out and down the path away from them.

"Oh, thank God. It was just a cat." She shook her head while palming her heart.

"That's Sylvester the farm cat. We have about five that roam the property. Feral cats," he added.

"I guess I'm just a little jumpy after you mentioned coyotes and bears. I'm sorry. I don't mean to be such a girl," she said, trying to hide her silly side.

"No worries. It's a lot different living out here than in Philly." They stopped at the barn door.

"Good night. Thanks again for a great dinner tonight. And thanks for walking us home." She placed a hand on the wooden frame and yanked it open.

John caught the door in his hands and held it steady. "Any time. I enjoyed the company. And I think Sheba did as well."

She entered the barn, turning slightly and looking over her shoulder. "See ya," she said.

"Don't forget to bolt the door shut from the inside."

A silly giggle escaped her lips as she made her way over to the door. Once he closed it, she slid the bolt across and latched it. They'd made an agreement she would come down each morning and unlatch the door by six thirty a.m. That way, the workers or himself could get inside and get the tools and tractor out. She was up early anyway. Fluffy had to go out and relieve himself, so it worked out.

After she got up to the loft, she gave Fluffy some water and changed into her comfy bedtime attire. She slipped under the covers, closing her eyes for a moment. When she opened them, it was after six a.m., and Fluffy was sitting by the front door, waiting patiently for her to take him outside.

CHAPTER 4

She had a busy schedule for the day. So, after a quick breakfast and a cup of coffee, she made the second cup in her to-go cup, and off she and Fluffy went. Today's travels would take them the furthest. Three villages over, and her maximum number of miles she said she'd drive to groom. When she pulled up to the sprawling ranch, for a fleeting moment she wondered who lived in this beautiful piece of real estate. A doctor perhaps? Maybe a lawyer.

She glanced around the sprawling house and property as she made her way to the porch. She was ready to knock when the door flew open, and two cocker spaniels rushed out barking.

"Sorry. They won't bite. They're just a bit noisy is all. Please come in."

"Is it okay for Fluffy to come too?" Maddy smiled down at him, then met the lady's gaze.

"Sure. Come on in."

"Something smells so wonderful in here," Maddy said as she followed the cheerful woman.

"Thank you. I've been baking all morning for the craft and bake sale. By the way, I'm Margorie Schneider." She reached out her hand to Maddy.

"Maddy Pryor."

"I've heard all about you. Folks around here are really happy with your mobile service."

"That's good news. I love dogs." She raised her shoulders to her ear and grinned.

"Buffy needs a bath desperately. And her nails trimmed."

"I can do that. I'll get started right now." She crouched down and whistled for Buffy to come to her. She called her by name and snapped her fingers. Buffy didn't budge.

"She thinks she's going to get a shot or something." Margorie moved toward Buffy and leaned over to get her. In a flash, the dog took off and started running around the kitchen in circles, cutting around the table like she was barrel racing.

"Oh, I can see. She is so funny. Look at her go." Maddy bobbled her head, watching her run.

Finally, Margorie cornered Buffy and grabbed her. Maddy widened her eyes when she heard a growl escaped the dog's mouth. Margorie tapped her on the nose. "Stop it this instant," she scolded.

Maddy reached for her and took her out of Margorie's arms. She began to speak softly and do a little baby talk to poor Buffy, who was shaking unmercifully.

"I'll have her back in an hour or so."

Buffy wasn't the most cooperative dog she'd ever groomed. But at least she didn't bite her, although the low belly growl kept Maddy on her toes. When she delivered her back to Margorie, Buffy couldn't even wait for her mommy to inspect her. She hightailed it out of sight to a back room.

"How did she do?" Margorie's soft brown eyes held concern and worry.

"She did okay. It wasn't her most favorite thing to do, for sure."

The woman dug into her purse and withdrew money. "I know you said forty dollars, but here's a tip. Since Buffy wasn't so nice."

"Ah, thank you so much."

"And, would you like some baked goodies? It seems I made too much." She walked over to the counter where dozens of wrapped items sat.

"Sure. I never turn down food, especially sweets."

She loaded her up with some cupcakes, a pumpkin roll, and some homemade fudge.

"I will never keep my girlish figure if I keep eating like this," Maddy said, sniffing the sugary delights.

"I wish I had a girlish figure to keep. Mine vanished years ago." Margorie chuckled.

Maddy took her loot back to the van and got Fluffy situated for the ride home. It was a successful first appointment, even if the client wasn't very willing.

She couldn't resist sampling the goodies as she drove to each appointment. By the time they'd gotten home, almost all the fudge was gone, and Maddy sensed a small bellyache coming on.

Covered in fur, she couldn't wait to get a shower and find a movie to watch. But they had one more grooming to do. The address the woman had given her over the phone didn't exist. Maddy drove around a little more before calling the client back.

The woman laughed and apologized for getting the numbers mixed up. Maddy told her she'd be on the way and took off to find the right house. When the van pulled in, a pack of dogs circled her van, showing teeth and barking. Maddy couldn't help but feel a bit intimidated. Buffy wasn't anything compared to this. She sat in her van, contemplating what to do when a woman ran out of the house with a broom to shoo them off. They listened to her and ran toward the back of the small house. Maddy slowly rolled down her window.

"Sorry about that. They're my guard dogs."

"Yeah, I see."

"My little Jazzy is in the house. She's the one I want you to groom."

"I have to tell you…I'm a bit scared right now to get out of my van. I have my own dog to worry about as well." Maddy looked away toward where the dogs ran off.

"They won't bother you. I promise."

Being new to the community and all, Maddy wasn't sure what to believe. Granted, most people had been helpful and kind. But something about this old woman struck a chord with Maddy, and she wasn't getting out of her van. She hit the door locks.

The woman insisted everything would be alright.

"Just get out of your van and follow closely behind me. I won't let anything happen to you."

"Momma! What in the world are you doing?"

Maddy whirled around to see where the man's voice was coming from. There, coming at a fast pace was a man. Maddy started to roll up the windows and put the van in gear.

"No, don't leave," the woman yelled.

Maddy pulled the van away from the screaming woman just as the woman raised her broom to hit the side. Her son yanked at his mother's arm, and she whirled around and began hitting him with the broom. Buffy started barking, and Maddy drove as fast as she could back to her loft.

John was sitting out on the rockers with all his fur family around him. He waved and smiled. She was happy to see him, especially after the day she'd had. She came to a stop, gathered some baked goodies and Fluffy, and crossed over to the porch.

"Hello, Maddy."

"Hey, John."

"Have a seat. Rest your feet."

She plopped down in the rocking chair next to him. After Fluffy greeted his friends, he rested on the porch floor, licking his paws like a cat.

"Here, this is for you." Maddy handed him the pumpkin roll.

"Margorie Schneider?"

"How'd you guess?"

"The craft and bake sale is coming up. She always makes too much."

"I ate a pound of fudge today." Maddy lowered her gaze and rocked.

"I feel your pain. I've done it too." He laughed and rocked too.

"I don't know if mobile grooming is my calling." She blurted out the statement without any follow-up.

"You love dogs, though. You have patience," John said.

"What can you tell me about the older woman out on Prospect Street. Has a pack of angry dogs."

John leaned forward and stared at her. "No. Tell me you didn't go there."

"She called and made an appointment. I should have known something was up. She gave me the wrong address."

"She doesn't live there. That's her son's house. He's not cooking on all four burners either."

"What's her story?" Maddy rested her head back on the chair and rocked, the sounds of the chair on the porch making her feel at ease.

"She lives at the dementia facility. She was only visiting. Those dogs...they are a pack of angry dogs. They run loose all over his property. Some say he's doing illegal stuff out there. I'm glad you're safe."

"Illegal stuff! Like what?"

"Drugs. But I don't know for sure. It could also be stolen stuff. We just know he's very secretive, has money yet doesn't work, doesn't farm, well, unless it's drugs, and we all just stay as far away from him as possible."

Maddy sighed. "Yeah, like I said, not convinced the grooming business is for me." She stood.

"Going already?" He stopped rocking and stood.

"I want a hot shower, a bowl of ramen, and I'm going to fall into bed."

"After a good night's sleep, you'll feel better about your career choice. Maybe we can have dinner again. I enjoyed your company."

"Sure. See you around, John."

Possibly, mobile dog grooming wasn't her calling. She'd done a lot of soul-searching, especially after the pack of dogs almost ate her and Fluffy for breakfast. The money was good, but she'd have to do about eight dogs every single day to pay the bills. She was the sole provider. Perhaps she should find something else to do. But what?

She couldn't bake. She couldn't cook. She wasn't really fond of children. Dogs. She loved dogs. That sort of limits you when you don't have any skills. She stood at the sink and washed out the bowl she had her soup in, and the spoon, and set them in the dish drainer. It was also getting kind of lonely living out in the sticks. She knew she wanted to get away from the city, but the truth of the matter was, she missed the city lights, the hustle and bustle, and the food. What she'd do for a tomato pie, or an Italian hoagie smothered in peppers and onion. "I think a trip to see Grandma and Grandpa is in order." Her gaze lowered to a sleeping Fluffy.

She hit the call button and listened to the ring. When her cheery mom answered, Maddy felt immediately better. Her mother always made her smile.

"Hey, Mom. How are you?"

"We're good, how about you?"

"I thought I'd come home next weekend. I have to finish up all my grooming appointments for this week, but then I'm free."

"Wonderful. We'll look forward to seeing you. Is there anything you're hungry for? I'm sure living out in the boonies, you don't get your favorites."

Maddy widened her grin. Her mom always knew what to say too.

MADDY INFORMED John she and Fluffy would be away for a few days. She cleared her calendar while she decided what she was going to do. Her rent was month to month, so getting out of paying it would be a breeze.

"Is everything okay?" he asked.

"Yeah. Why wouldn't it be?" She toned down the

defensiveness gradually. She didn't have a beef with him. She actually liked him. No sense in burning bridges.

"I just haven't seen you around is all. The van has stayed parked for the past couple of days."

"Oh, about that. I didn't book any appointments so I could get out of town. We've just been hanging out in the loft."

He reared his head back and leveled a wary stare toward her.

The way he scrutinized her made her feel like a kid who'd just got caught with her hand in the cookie jar.

"Just wanted to make certain. If there's anything I can do, just ask. By the way, Sheba could use a bath and haircut. Can you squeeze her in when you return from Philly?"

"Absolutely," she said, not wanting to divulge she may be giving up the grooming business altogether.

"Have fun. Eat some pizza, and let's see…hoagies." He turned and strolled away.

She couldn't just leave without saying something positive about Lancaster County, even though she wasn't feeling the same way about it.

"Enjoy the peace and quiet of the country. I'll be listening to honking horns, blaring music, and loud-mouth tourists." She flashed him a smile.

He turned back to face her, walking backward. "You

can leave all of that there when you come back." He winked.

She wasn't sure how she felt about the wink. Was that a sign of flirting, or just his way of being cute. Either way, she kind of liked it.

SHE ROSE EARLY, ensuring Fluffy had his outside time before they hit the road to Philly. The lights in the house were on, and she could see movement through the sheers hanging in the windows, the backdrop of the room dimly lit, casting a warm yellow glow. John was up before the cows were. Literally.

Tossing a large ziplock bag with Fluffy's food and her favorite pillow she could not get a good night's rest without into her duffel-style bag, she lifted her furry companion into the van and slid into the driver's seat. As she rounded the corner and drove by his house, her gaze drew to a man walking toward the dairy barn. Dressed in jeans, a lightweight jacket, and boots, she could see the outline of his toned physique. Working on a farm proved to be quite the exercise. She pulled out of the driveway to the edge where it met the main road. She glanced up at her rearview mirror. She might just miss the place, or John even.

CHAPTER 5

The drive to see her parents was basically uneventful. Unless you count forgetting her razor and her earbuds. She stopped at the large discount store right outside town to pick up the items. She didn't often keep Fluffy inside the van alone, but the temperatures outside were cool. Fall was definitely in the air. She jogged up to the automatic doors and went inside. She headed straight to the cosmetic area, her gaze landing on her brand of razors. Then she headed over to electronics. As she searched the pegs holding various brands and price ranges, she heard a woman berating someone. Telling them they were no good, never would amount to anything, and when she heard the slap, she whirled around. Just then, a young child cried out. Maddy's jaw dropped, and before she realized it, she rushed to the child, pulling her up out of the shopping cart. The woman shot daggers at Maddy.

"That's my child. Get your hands off of her."

"You just slapped her. Not to mention the belittling. What is your problem, lady?" Maddy shot the wicked look right back at her.

"I can discipline my child the way I and my maker see fit." She looked up.

"Your maker? Does he tell you to slap your child and call her names? I don't think so. Not my God anyway. There's a special place in hell for those who beat on children and animals. I hope you have a nice trip." She walked off, still holding the child.

The woman grabbed Maddy by the hair and tugged so hard it made her almost drop the child.

"Help. Someone, help me," Maddy screamed.

Several store clerks who were stocking shelves nearby came running. With wide eyes and blustery cheeks, one of the heavier men asked them what in the world was going on.

"This woman was hitting on her child and talking so nasty to her. I want to report her to the police."

"She kidnapped my baby," the woman wailed.

"Call security, now," Maddy demanded.

Two men in vests with the store logo approached her. "Ma'am, please come with us."

"What about her?" Maddy asked, her brows dipping inward.

"My associate will take care of her. Please hand over the child back to its mother."

"Are you serious? This woman was abusing her child."

The associate took the little girl out of Maddy's arms and gave her back.

The little girl leaned out of her mother's arms and screamed, "No."

Worried Fluffy would start getting antsy in the van, Maddy told the security employees she couldn't stay. They looked at her as if she'd said something in a foreign language.

"Seriously. My dog is out in my van. I just ran in here to get two items when that lunatic of a mother started in on her defenseless child. I didn't kidnap her. I tried to get her to safety."

The small room they took her to held a table and four chairs. It reminded her of an interrogation room she'd seen on a detective show. A rap on the door made her and the employee look over. The second security associate came through the door. He whispered something in the other's ear. Maddy could hear rumblings but couldn't make out the exact words. The two men stepped out, leaving her alone.

Shoving back into the chair, she crossed her arms. "This is ridiculous," she said under her breath.

The door flew open, and the police walked in. The officer adjusted the volume on his walkie-talkie and sat. "Maddy Pryor?"

"Yes. I'd never hurt that child. The opposite is true. Her mother was slapping her and verbally abusing her. I was just—"

The police officer drew a finger to his mouth. "Stop talking. It's all been sorted out. You're a hero."

Maddy dropped back into the chair, her shoulders sagging. "I am?"

"That woman kidnapped that child. Her mother was on the other side of the store, frantically searching for her. She'd left her sitting in the cart while she tried on some clothes. When she came out, the child and the cart were missing."

"How'd you find that out?"

"Just about the time your situation was unfolding, the woman had gone up to the customer service desk to report her child missing. Anyway, she's back to her mother, and the woman is under arrest. You're free to go." He pushed back his chair and stood.

"Thank you. This is not exactly how I envisioned my trip would be. I'm headed into Philly to see my folks. I ran in here to pick up two items. I'm not even all that fond of kids."

"Well, go ahead and finish your shopping. I'm sorry for the detainment. But you saved a little girl today from God knows what. You were in the right place at the right time."

"I'm glad." She walked to the door. "I felt like something wasn't right. I guess it pays to be observant."

"See something, say something." The officer followed her out.

After her ordeal, she just wanted to get to Fluffy. She'd get the razors and earbuds later.

She pulled open the side door. Fluffy wagged his tail then barked.

"I'm sorry, boy. I had a situation. Let's get back on the road." She petted him on the head.

EXHAUSTED BY THE ORDEAL, Maddy drove the rest of the way to her parents' in a daze. Her parents were happy to see her. She'd only been gone a couple of months, yet her folks seemed to have aged. How could that be? But being the only child of older parents, she'd always known her relationship was unique with them. They were soft-spoken, went to bed early, rose early, and always had a pot of coffee going—for those unexpected neighbor drop-ins. She filled up Fluffy's water bowl and set it out of the way. He lapped and lapped until he drooled all over her mom's freshly mopped linoleum. Pulling off a couple of sheets from the paper towel roll, Maddy soaked up the slobber. "Sorry about that, Mom."

"No problem, dear. Fluffy is a thirsty boy."

The three of them sat at the old chrome and laminate table her mom inherited from her late aunt. She hated to part with it because, one, it was in great condition, and two, the memories it held. Maddy assured her she'd not be so sentimental about some old table.

They chatted about her ordeal at the store. Her mother's jaw dropped. Her father sputtered and then carefully began talking. "I'm just glad you're okay, Maddy." His eyes twinkled as he patted her hand.

Having older parents worked in her favor a lot. They were easily entertained, didn't seem to get too excited about anything, including their only daughter almost getting arrested, and like the saying, nothing ruffled their feathers, it was so very true.

"Thought we'd go have pizza and beer for dinner, Maddy," her dad said, changing the subject.

That's what she loved about Richard and Emma Jean Pryor. No reason to beat a dead horse. They'd moved on. Now they were talking about real issues. Food, what's for dinner, food.

"That sounds great. My mouth has been watering for some good pizza."

"Don't they have that in Amish country?" Her mom busied herself at the counter.

"Not really. It's more like comfort food there."

"*Pizza* is comfort food," Richard said.

"What is it you're doing out there anyway?" Emma Jean asked.

"Mobile grooming," Maddy said, taking a bite out of a homemade oatmeal cookie.

"That's right," Emma Jean said, wiping down the counter.

"Mom, just say it. Don't beat around the bush."

Emma Jean turned, resting her hips against the cabinet. "I just don't understand why you had to go so far away."

"It's just a couple of hours up the road. Lancaster County."

"I know, but we miss you."

"I had to get out of here. Clear my head. Ryan really messed me over."

"I still can't believe he kicked our sweet boy." Richard gazed over to Fluffy, now curled up on the braided oval rug near the door.

"I can't either. But it just wasn't how he treated Fluffy," Maddy said under her breath.

"He better not have kicked you." Richard puffed out his chest.

"No, it was more verbal abuse."

"That's all in the past, dear. Just come home," Emma Jean pleaded.

"I'm happy right now in Lancaster. I have a great landlord. John."

"Is he an Amish farmer?" her dad asked.

"A dairy farmer. Plus, he grows vegetables."

"And you're sleeping in a barn?" Her mother crossed her arms, leaning back against the counter.

"Not a barn, Mom. In a loft inside the barn."

Emma Jean furrowed her brows.

"Come out and visit me. It's a nice drive. They are gearing up for a big fall festival. The corn stalks are huge, and the homemade bakery goods are so yummy. The air is crisp and fresh, you'd love it," she sang.

"Okay. We'll do that. Perhaps in a couple of weeks?" Emma's eyes met Richard's.

Richard rotated his hand around his stomach. "Ready for that pizza yet?" When he laughed, his belly shook.

"You know your father. He never misses a meal."

"Let me freshen up first." Maddy slid her chair back.

John and she had exchanged cell numbers. They had to. Landlord-tenant stuff. But when she pulled up her contacts, and his name showed up, a little part of her wanted to call him. But what would she say? She'd have to be clever. She couldn't let on she'd already missed him. That would just be plain crazy. And she'd already seen and heard crazy once today. At the store. She shuddered. Yeah, maybe one crazy thing is enough for this day. She exited out of her contact list and tossed her phone into her crossover bag.

CHAPTER 6

The weekend getaway was just what Maddy needed. She'd gotten her fill of pizza, hoagies, her mother's scrapple, and of course, their love. No matter how old Maddy was, she always needed their love and approval.

Loaded down with items from their cupboards, Maddy kissed them both on the cheek as she and Fluffy headed out.

"We'll see you in a couple of weeks. I have a doctor's appointment to check out this bunion on my foot," Richard said.

"And don't forget the luncheon at the church," Emma Jean said, tipping her chin toward her husband.

Maddy nodded. "Okay, I'll see you when you can make it. Just give me a couple days' notice."

"Don't stop at any stores. Go straight to your loft," her dad yelled.

"Yes, Dad." The corners of her mouth drew up.

As she drove out of the city, her heart raced a bit. Lancaster County was calling her. Or perchance it was John?

Maddy had been driving for almost two hours, daydreaming to make the trip go by faster. Was mobile grooming really her calling? Possibly she wasn't looking deep enough. The music in the van was blaring. An old, favorite tune of hers came on, and she couldn't resist turning it up. Bobbing her head and tapping her fingers to the steering wheel, she sang along as they wheeled down the highway. But when the sounds of sirens broke into her song, her gaze flew immediately to the rearview mirror. "Police. Yikes." Realizing he was after her, she pulled over to the side of the road. She rolled down the window and watched as the uniformed officer made his way to her.

"Driver's license, please."

She couldn't see his eyes for the dark sunglasses. "Yes, sir." She turned to her purse. Fluffy barked.

"Contain your dog, ma'am."

"He's friendly. He's just a little startled is all." She handed him her license.

"Just a second." He walked away with her license.

"Be quiet, Fluffy," Maddy said, shaking a finger at him.

"Okay, ma'am," the officer said, handing her back her license. "Were you aware you were going twenty over the speed limit?"

"No, sir." She didn't really know, to be truthful. But that sounded fair enough.

"Yes. I could give you a ticket. But I'm going to let you off with a warning."

"Thank you, sir. I'm just a bit anxious to get home is all."

"Where you headed?"

"Lancaster County. I live on the property of John Cooper's dairy farm. I'm almost home."

"John Cooper, huh?"

"Yes. Do you know him?"

"He's my brother-in-law."

Maddy gulped. Brother-in-law? That's right. He was married. Her jaw fell agape.

"John is sweet. He's very lonely. He misses your sister so much."

"My sister? No, his sister is my wife."

"Silly me. I shouldn't have assumed. You know what they say about assuming," she said, rattling on now, trying to hide her embarrassment.

"No worries. Have a good day. And remember, do the speed limit. The next time you might not be so lucky." He turned up the corners of his mouth and flashed her a smile.

"Thank you," she replied.

So, John has a sister. Married to a Pennsylvania state police officer. Interesting.

When Maddy pulled into the dairy farm, she could see workers in and around the barn as well as out in the cornfields. The stalks must have grown two feet just in a few days. Fall was definitely in the air, and she wondered what types of activities this little Amish community had planned. No doubt apple strudel and other homemade goodies.

Passing by the main house, two buggies were parked nearby. She slowed down as she went around them, taking care not to spook the horses. She briefly looked around but didn't see the owners of the buggies. Maybe they were in the house.

Maddy gathered her overnight bag and Fluffy and took the steps to her cozy loft over the tool barn. It felt a bit stuffy inside, so she opened the one large sliding window to let the fresh air in. Soon the lacy curtains whipped around as the breeze blew in. She'd just kicked her shoes off and bounced on the bed when a light rap on her door had her standing back up.

She should have known it would be him. Who else knew she lived above the tractors?

"Did you have a nice visit with your folks?" He pulled off his baseball cap and ran his fingers through his hair before placing it back on his head.

"I did. It was nice. Mom and Dad spoiled me. It was just what the doctor ordered to chase my blues away. Would you like to come in?" She stepped back away from the door opening.

"No, I just wanted to pop up and say hi. I heard you met my brother-in-law?" His eyes crinkled, and Maddy found herself mesmerized by the coolness of his blue eyes.

"Yes." She laughed it off.

"He's a great guy. My sister is fortunate to have him in her life. Or so she tells me." He shrugged.

"It sure is a beautiful day. I can feel fall in the air. And those corn stalks. Wow, they grew overnight." She loved the way she could change a subject without missing a beat. It was something she did well.

"Most of it is for feed, but I like to let the community enjoy it during fall festival time. We'll make a maze, and the kiddos will have a blast. The womenfolk come out here and set up stands selling their homemade bakery items. They'll have some traditional foods from their culture and some favorites everyone loves. You should visit during it. We have a lot of fun."

"You really fit in here, don't you?" She grabbed the threshold with one hand and leaned in with her head cocked slightly.

"I had no choice," he said, turning somewhat away.

"No choice. What do you mean?"

"My wife grew up here. Anyway, back to work. See you around."

"Hey, John," she called out.

He pivoted to meet her gaze.

"Let's have dinner again. Soon."

He dipped his fingers into the pockets of his washed-out blue jeans. "That would be nice."

CHAPTER 7

Pushing the door shut, Maddy leaned her back up against it. She watched as the curtains danced in the breeze. She found herself wanting to get inside John's head. Why though?

Maddy had a full schedule of baths and nail clippings to keep her busy. She met some nice folks, some standoffish ones, and some who could have been her grandparents. All of them with a story of love and how they came about being parents to a four-legged creature. She enjoyed listening to all the rescue stories, and when it was time to leave after visiting with her oldest clients, they did what most grandmotherly types would do. They loaded her up on goodies.

She'd noticed her expanding waistline just that morning while squeezing into her jeans, thanks to the homemade items. She needed to add some exercise to her routine, but after a long day grooming, all she wanted to do was watch a good flick on her tablet.

But she did what her parents raised her to do; she thanked them and took them, only later to devour them.

The buggies were in front of John's house again. Maddy's nosey side, the one she got from her mother, couldn't let her rest without knowing why they visited so often. She understood they were a close-knit community, but John wasn't Amish.

She parked her van and got out. She'd just drop in for a second. Give him some treats she'd taken from the old women. She rapped on his door. She could hear rumblings from inside, then sounds of boots on hardwood moving closer to the door.

"Maddy," he said, looking back over his shoulder.

She peered around him and saw two men standing in the background, wearing dark clothes and hats. "Hey. I just was on my way home and thought I'd share this with you." She handed him the bundles wrapped in foil and cellophane.

He took the baked items. "Thanks. Ah, maybe we can talk later. I have company right now."

His bewildered look made her uneasy. As if she'd intruded. Not at all what she wanted to feel. "Sure." She stepped back. "Come up when you get a chance. We have a dinner date, remember?" She flashed him an awkward grin.

"Okay, Maddy. Thanks again for the food."

He'd turned up the volume on that last line, causing Maddy to frown. She clearly wasn't feeling the warm and cozy friendship she'd felt before with him. Something was up. He didn't want those men to know anything about her, apparently. She picked up her hand and waved. "See you around," she mumbled.

That was odd. Shaking her head, she climbed back into the driver's seat and drove around the back to her place. "Men. I can't figure them out, Fluffy."

MADDY POPPED the cork to a bottle of wine she'd been saving. *Saving for what?* She poured the dark red liquid and held the glass to her nose. Notes of cherry, vanilla, and spices wafted up to her nose. She drew in a taste and swirled it around in her mouth before swallowing. Pulling open the small refrigerator door, she peeked inside. Ramen was getting old, even for Maddy. Opening the crisper drawer, she retrieved a block of cheese. Moving to the cupboard, she took out a box of crackers. Dinner would be snacks. And wine. Lots of wine.

Nestling under the covers with her tablet, she found a romance movie and began to watch. The couple had angst, turmoil, conflict, and more. Then they made up, broke up, only to get together again. Talk about an emotional roller coaster. When the ending came, and they pledged their undying love for all eternity, tears began to roll down Maddy's face. Sniffling back the tears, she closed her tablet. "Romance. Who needs it?"

Snuggling deeper, she closed her eyes. The wine had clearly gone to her head, and sleep was about to overcome her. And it did. When she woke, it was in the morning, and sunlight peeked through the curtains at her, making her shield her eyes.

After coffee and homemade cinnamon rolls dripping in gooey frosting, she dressed in a grooming smock and jeans and, together with Fluffy, hit the road. She had some new customers and a few returning. All in all, another full day of toenail clippings, dog fur, and the occasional whimper, a sometimes-low growl, in the name of dog grooming, but still unsure if it was the right calling for her. She found herself daydreaming when combing out Pippi, the poodle, or when trimming the tail of Callie, the Pomeranian. And of course, John entered her brain too.

The low hum of the electric razor as Maddy gently guided it down the back of Pippi made the little dog shake. She tried to reassure her it would be okay by baby talking to her as she worked. The apricot poodle with the grooming loop around its neck stood, but Maddy knew from experience, grooming sessions wore out dogs, and Pippi would not be the exception. She ran the brush around her legs, fluffing out the fur before trimming. And when Pippi was finished, Maddy tied a bandanna around her neck and spritzed on some doggy cologne in a few places.

Maddy lifted the little dog down from the table, placing her in a holding cage while she cleaned up. When she finished, she took the dog back to her owner, where she didn't waste any time running into her house and as far away as she could from Maddy and her shears.

"Thank you," Maddy told the lady as she folded the bills and slipped them in the pocket of her smock. "See you in five weeks."

On the way home, Maddy stopped at the local market to pick up a few items. Perhaps she'd surprise John with dinner. She looked around the store when she found a sign that said take-home casseroles. Now that was something she could do. She scrutinized various foil containers. Homemade chicken pot pie. The directions said 350 degrees for thirty minutes. She took one and placed it in her carry basket. She found a premade salad with bacon bits and dried cranberries. She checked the expiration date before tossing it into the basket. And to finish off this surprise dinner, a slice of carrot cake that could feed four found its way into Maddy's basket as well.

When she drove onto the long drive of the dairy, her gaze immediately went to the black buggy near the house. *That's strange.* Almost every day, that buggy was there. Or perchance it was a different buggy each day. She slowed to almost a crawl as she passed by John's house. No sign of anything going on. She parked the van in front of the tool barn and gathered her things. She'd wait until his guest was gone. The last time she made an appearance at his doorstep when he had a visitor, he got a bit anxious.

Maddy tried to be as inconspicuous as possible. She walked Fluffy out around the fenced-in area where the corn was growing. The workers had left for the day. She heard a few cows mooing in the other barn and decided to check it out. All lined up, swatting their tails with their heads stuck into their feed bins, Maddy watched with a grin. Some of the cow's udders were full. She thought about that for a second. How uncomfortable that must be. Then she laughed.

At that moment, she heard the wheels of the buggy clop along as it rode out. She hurried out to see them leave just in time to make eye contact with the driver. He was probably in his sixties, wearing the traditional overalls, white long-sleeve shirt, and a big-brimmed hat. He held the reins as he guided the horses. The man tipped his head at her. A funny feeling came over Maddy. The Amish folks were nice enough but so mysterious in many ways.

She looked over to John's porch and found him standing, staring at the buggy as it traveled further away. She yelled out a hello to him.

"Hey," he said.

"Boy, you are sure popular."

He pulled his brows together. "Popular?"

"Every day you have an Amish guest."

"Oh. That."

"Listen, I stopped in at the local market and picked up a chicken pot pie and a salad. Would you like to have dinner with me?" Maddy reached down and petted Fluffy, smiling up at him.

"I see you discovered the take-home casseroles. They are really good. I've had a few of them. Sure. Want to bring it over here and bake it?"

"Okay. I'll go grab the stuff and see you in fifteen minutes or so."

She rushed back to the loft, pulling Fluffy along, not letting him stop and smell some of his special spots along the way. "Come on, boy. You can stop and sniff another time."

She washed her hands and clutched the grocery bag still sitting on her table. At the last minute, she decided to bring Fluffy. He got along so well with Sheba.

John must have seen her walk up.

"Come in. The door is open."

She opened the screen door and entered. She went straight back to the kitchen.

"I've preheated the oven for you."

"Great." She took the items out of the bag and set them on the counter.

"Let me get a cookie sheet to place that on. In case it bubbles over." He looked inside a lower cupboard, retrieving a shiny tray.

"And a bowl for the salad," Maddy said.

He opened another cabinet and brought out a large plastic bowl. He tore open the bag and let the contents fall into the bowl.

As the pot pie baked, they enjoyed a glass of wine and visited.

"You have a lot of Amish friends, don't you?" she asked.

"I do. Some work for me. I think I mentioned that to you before." He tapped his fingers on the counter.

"I hope you don't think I'm being too nosey. The Amish folks intrigue me. They're so quiet."

"Yes, they are. They don't do a lot of talking, only when they're spoken to," he said.

"Do you know a lot about them? Their culture?" She raised the glass to her mouth.

"I do."

"I'm—"

The beep of the oven timer went off, stopping her in midstream.

She'd reserve her question for later. She was just getting some answers to her questions. John wasn't telling her everything…or was he?

He jumped up and grabbed the oven mitts, pulling open the oven door. She moved near him to help. He had it all under control, though. He'd been single for a while. Maybe he'd always loved to cook.

"Looks great, smells even better," he said, placing the hot pie on a trivet to cool.

"I may never cook again," she said.

He tossed her a funny look.

"Learn to cook," she corrected then laughed.

He served up two helpings while she tossed the salad. They took turns blowing on forked bites before devouring the savory chicken dish.

"I don't think I've ever tasted anything so yummy,"

she said, appreciating the rich gravy and chunks of white chicken breast.

"So, as I was saying before the timer went off. The Amish community is new for me. I mean, I knew of them, and I've been to Lancaster County before, but never lived amongst them."

"They'd give you the shirt off their back. I don't know where'd I be without them. After my wife died, they came to my house and brought me food for weeks. The women cleaned the house, the men took care of the cows and the farm. They let me grieve and took care of me."

She set her fork down and pushed her plate away, leaving room to rest her hands. "They sound like wonderful people. What was your wife's name?"

"Sarah."

"Sarah," she repeated.

He slid his chair back and began to pick up their plates. "Coffee?"

"Sure," she said, watching him with a careful eye as he prepared the coffee.

"Was Sarah from Lancaster?"

He didn't answer her but instead began to rinse off the dishes as the brown liquid dripped into the glass carafe.

"I was just curious," she said, feeling awkward for the

intrusion.

Drying his hands off, he retrieved two cups from the cabinet.

"My former boyfriend is from Philly."

John paused, then began to pour their coffee.

She moved to the counter and sliced the huge piece of cake into two and placed one on each plate he'd set next to it. Recalling the drawer where he kept the silverware, Maddy opened it and brought out two forks.

Carrying the cups, he moved to the table and set them down. She followed him with the cake.

"I hope you don't think I'm being too forward. I just thought it would be nice to get to know one another better." She lifted the cup to her mouth, smelling the aroma before tasting. "Coffee is good," she added.

"Uh-huh," he said.

"Look, maybe I should leave. Clearly, I've overstepped my bounds here." She set the cup down and moved her chair back, her hand sliding off the table as the chair moved.

He quickly placed his hand on hers, stopping it. "Don't go."

John's eyes drew her back, and soon she was scooting her chair forward. "You must understand. I loved my wife with all of my heart. We were devastated when she got the news of cancer. Devastated because I knew what she was going to go through, but also because I'd have to watch it. I hoped I would be strong enough for us both. It was rough, though. When you love someone that much, seeing them in pain, going through hell each and every day, and yet, smiling at you, trying to bring cheer to you, instead of the other way around, that was so hard." He hung his head.

She rested her hand on his. The warmth of his skin gave her the courage to speak candidly.

"Your love for her is admirable. Not every man has such deep love for their partner. My parents do, but I've never been fortunate enough to have that kind of relationship. I can't imagine what you've been through. Just talking about it with you has touched my heart," she said, speaking softly.

He nodded, then quickly wiped the stray tear away.

"It's okay to grieve for her. You'll always love her and miss her. That's what true love is." She patted his hand.

"Thank you," he said.

"John?"

He looked up.

"I know a little about the Amish, but as I said earlier, not as much as I'd like to. I've read some stories in magazines about kids who run off from the community and never come back. Do you know anyone that has done that?"

She waited for his answer.

"That's a bizarre thing to ask me." He drew his hand away.

"I... I'm sorry. I didn't mean to strike a nerve."

"I have an early morning tomorrow. Many of the cows need milking, and it's time to harvest the corn."

"I thought you were making a maze?"

"We are. I'll harvest some, leaving the rest. Thanks for dinner. Next time, I'll put something together to pay you back."

"No need to repay me. That's what friends do." She snapped her fingers for Fluffy to come. He'd been sleeping next to his new friend, Sheba.

She made her way to his front door, turning around at the last moment before exiting, her gaze meeting his.

"John. I'm sorry if I brought up a sensitive subject. Our conversation won't go anywhere but here. I promise."

"Good night, Maddy. Thanks again for dinner…and the company. I do appreciate it. Maybe in time, I can let you in on more, but for now, that's all I can share."

Maddy walked back to her loft in a daze. He led her to believe he liked her. At least that's what she thought. But he was secretive. It was what made him so interesting. The allure of the unknown. And it didn't hurt he was handsome, his build lean and mean, and those eyes.

Like waves of the ocean surrounded by white clouds. Sighing, she dropped her shoulders and kept walking. He was hiding something. That was the only thing she could be positive about.

CHAPTER 8

Maddy woke up with a slight headache and an irritating cough. Putting one leg out from under the covers, then the other, she sat upright, rubbing her arms. Blinking a few times to try to focus, she grabbed her head with her hands and moaned. She was sick.

Stumbling out of bed, she made her way to the kitchen, looking for something to soothe her throat and make her headache go away. And since she didn't know how to cook, homemade chicken soup, which sounded divine about now, would be out of the question for her to find stocked in her fridge. She pulled open the cabinet door and selected chicken-flavored ramen. It would have to do.

While the water boiled in the microwave for the

ramen, she put her cup under the Keurig and hit the hot water button for tea. Thank goodness she had some lemon herbal tea. That might soothe her what was once just a scratchy, irritating cough to a full-blown sore throat. In a matter of seconds too!

Slurping on her soup and tea, alternatively, she began to feel a bit better. She flipped through her calendar on her phone. "Four appointments today. Ugh." She went through the contacts list and started with her first appointment. As she went down the list, she told each one the same thing. "I'm sorry to have to cancel, but I'm really not feeling well."

And as she figured, most people were understanding and even offered to bring her soup.

She shuffled back to bed and crawled under the covers. She'd just closed her eyes when Fluffy let out a shriek bark, drawing her straight up out of bed.

He began to whip his tail around and dance in circles. Maddy moaned and dropped back down, her head hitting the soft pillow. Fluffy let out another bark, then another, and finally, Maddy got up.

"Come on, boy. I know you must have to go potty."

She held on to the railing as she took the steps down. Wearing only her pajamas and a sweater she grabbed at the last minute, the two braved the brisk morning. Hunched over like an eighty-five-year-old woman,

Maddy let Fluffy sniff a bit before she ordered him to his business, and quickly.

With her hair strung down around her face, her frumpy clothes, and her unbrushed teeth, Maddy hoped to high heaven she didn't run into John. But you know what they say…

"Good morning," he called out, his chipper tone making her cringe.

"Morning," she whispered, trying to not breathe on him.

"You don't look so well."

"I woke up with a scratchy throat and a headache. My body aches everywhere too. I'm heading back to bed. Fluffy had to take care of business." She tugged on his leash and turned away from John.

"Can I bring you something. I have some homemade chicken soup."

She stopped and turned slightly. Homemade soup. Where was he a few minutes ago? "No, that's okay. I made some soup."

"Ramen?" He laughed.

"And lemon tea. I'll be fine. Thanks for your concern."

She took a step but stopped when she felt his hand on her back.

"Maddy. Let me bring you some soup for later. I promise it will cure all that ails you."

Soup did sound good. Especially homemade chicken. "All right. I might be asleep. Just come in and set it on the counter. But right now, I have to go before I hurl up the ramen right here." She grabbed her tummy.

"Sounds like the flu," he said.

Nodding, she moved away and made it back upstairs just in time. After heaving her guts out, she managed to keep down some water and finally crawled back into bed to sleep the morning away.

At some time during her sleep, John brought up the soap, some soda crackers, and a glass jar with purple stuff in it. She whiffed it, then tasted it. Berries of some sort. When she was feeling better, she called him.

"Thank you for the soup and crackers. What was the purple stuff in the jar?"

"That's elderberry syrup. Take some. You'll feel so much better."

"Elderberry syrup, huh?"

"Yes. I make several batches of it each year. I take a teaspoon daily and knock on wood, I've not gotten sick."

"Well, aren't you special. You make syrup to cure the flu, you cook like a chef, let's see, you milk your own cows and you grow your own food. You're like those Amish women." She laughed.

The pause on the other end unnerved her. She'd hit a chord or something, perhaps. She cleared her throat. "I'm sorry if that wasn't funny to you. It just came out."

"No worries. Just take some. I'll check in on you later."

She held the phone out from her ear. "He didn't say goodbye. I think I may have upset him, Fluffy." She tossed the phone on the table. Her gaze landed on the jar sitting on the table. She dipped a spoon into the liquid and swallowed it. Tasted good, she thought.

A LIGHT TAP on the door woke her up. "Come in," she yelled.

"How are you feeling?" John said, poking his head in.

She rubbed her eyes and yawned. "I feel pretty good, actually."

"Did you take the elderberry?"

"Yes, I did. I wasn't sure how often to take it, though."

"Take it about every six hours or so."

He backed out and began to close the door.

"Hey, John," she called out.

He opened the door and stepped in. "Yes?"

"Thanks for the soup and stuff. It really did taste

good. Much better than the ramen." She tried to wink, but it came off like she had something in her eye.

"No problem. Glad to help. Get some rest. You'll be good as new tomorrow."

"John. About the other night. I hope it doesn't change anything between us."

"No, why would it?" He narrowed his eyes.

"I just don't want you to think I'm prying into your business. I like to share. I guess that's one of my faults." She pulled the covers up to her neck.

"That's not a fault. If you feel comfortable enough to share, then that is probably a good thing."

She tipped her head. "Glad you feel that way. And then earlier when I made the Amish woman joke, it was in bad taste. I apologize for that."

"No worries. Talk to you later."

She lay back down and closed her eyes, the corners of her mouth drawn up in a half grin. "Well, he does act like an Amish woman," she said under her breath.

AFTER A DAY IN BED, sipping on hot tea and warmed chicken broth, Maddy began to feel better. She canceled her appointments for the day just to be sure she was well enough to resume her grooming duties. Standing at the sink, leaning her body up against the counter for support, she rinsed out her dishes, stacking them to dry. Her knees were wobbly from being in bed so long, and even though she'd eaten, her strength was that of an old woman. Not an old Amish woman, because those women could kick butt.

Thinking a shower and some clothes other than pajamas might make her feel better, too, Maddy stood under the head and let the water wash down all around her. She was feeling better already. She dressed in jeans and a flannel shirt, shoes and socks. She wasn't taking any chances of a relapse. Leashing up Fluffy, they made their way outdoors. The sun shone brightly through the remaining leaves that hadn't fallen, and the crisp air, believe it or not, made her feel alive. She'd felt like a zombie for two days, so this was refreshing.

Fluffy did his business, walking bush to bush, fence post to fence post. Maddy let him lead where his nose took him. After about twenty minutes, they headed back around the barn where the cows lived when they weren't outside. Mooing from the structure led her to peek inside.

She didn't know a lot about farming, but she did know that most dairies used machinery to milk cows. But not at John's. Lined up were stools with men sitting on them, milking the cows. Their gazes lifted to meet hers when she entered the barn. She flipped up her hand. "Hello," she said.

They turned back to what they were doing, not uttering a word. Rustling of leaves and crunching of gravel made her turn around. There standing behind her was John.

"Feeling better today?"

His happy grin was catchy, so she smiled back. "Yes, I am."

"Good. Glad to hear the elderberry syrup cured you." Another wide smile spread across his face.

She drew in a deep breath. "It's a beautiful day too. I was tired of being cooped up in the loft. Tomorrow I'll go back to grooming."

"It's always good to get back to your routine."

Just then, a cow mooed.

"Well, I guess we're disturbing them with our chatter," Maddy said.

"They do like their privacy." He chuckled.

They walked outside into the bright sunlight. He squinted then pulled his ball cap down to shield his eyes from some of it. Maddy's gaze floated from his face to his arms as he flexed his tan limb to adjust his hat.

"You're going to be seeing a lot of traffic here over the next few days. We got to get the maze ready for the little fall festival next week," he said.

Looking handsome as ever, Maddy stumbled for words. "That's right."

"The ladies of the community will be here with their menfolk, setting up the wooden structures. We'll be thinning out the crop to make the maze, and well, just lots of activity. I wanted you to know, in case you wanted to come outside in your pajamas to walk Fluffy." He regarded her steadily, making her pulse race.

"Oh, you've noticed, have you?" Her mouth widened, the corners lifting heavenward.

"It's hard not to. When a lady as lovely as yourself parades around in skimpy nightwear, who wouldn't look?"

Maddy pulled her lips in sharply and held them. She counted to three. "I'm not sure I like the way you said that. Come on, Fluffy."

Holding her head high, she marched off, leaving him behind.

The rest of the day, she tried her best to avoid him. Now he really was behaving like some Amish woman!

CHAPTER 9

Maddy fussed and fumed over John's statement. How dare he use the words lovely lady and skimpy in one sentence. She banged the cupboard door shut. Fluffy lay on his bed with his paws tucked under his chin, watching her every move, only blinking now and then as he eyed her.

"Don't worry, boy. I'm not mad at all of the male gender in this world. Only one." She plopped down on her bed and bounced. "I'm going to have to step up my game to let him see me as an equal. Not some bimbo that he apparently thinks I am." Rapping her fingers on her chin, she pondered what to do about him. If anything at all.

Later that day, during Fluffy's evening walk, she purposely moseyed around the cornfield. She thought maybe she'd run into him. Dressed appropriately in jeans and her flannel shirt from earlier, it clearly said conservative.

They locked eyes from a distance. She picked up her pace to meet him halfway. "Hey there, John."

"Twice in one day." He leaned over and petted Fluffy.

"I'm feeling better each hour. I have to tell you, that elderberry syrup is awesome."

"I've got to get back to work. Only a few more hours of daylight." He turned his back and began to walk away.

She'd had time to mull over his earlier statement, and perhaps he had a valid point. She wasn't just living on a deserted farm—there were workers, men, not to mention him. Trying to put her best foot forward, she decided hastily to make amends.

"About this morning," she blurted. "I don't normally dress like that. But Fluffy had to go, and I just wasn't using my head when I ventured outside."

He chuckled without turning around.

"I just don't want any bad blood between us. We just moved in and all," she mumbled.

Dipping his fingertips just inside his pockets, he shrugged. "No apology necessary."

She resisted the urge to say it wasn't she who should be apologizing. She didn't do anything wrong except come out in night clothes. But then again, this wasn't Philly.

"I was wondering…would you be free someday to teach me how to make the elderberry syrup?"

"Sure. In fact, I have some frozen berries from my last harvest. I tell you what, Sunday morning after you've walked Fluffy, come on over. How does that sound?" His wide smile was infectious.

Smiling back, she answered, "Sounds lovely."

THE REST of the week dragged on and on. Maddy couldn't believe how excited she was getting over making elderberry syrup. Maybe it wasn't the syrup that was getting her pulse racing and causing the hot flashes she couldn't explain. When Sunday came, she dressed in shorts and a tee shirt, and slipped on her favorite pair of flip-flops. Winding her straight hair around her fingers, she secured it with a clip and bounced out of the loft with Fluffy running behind.

She rapped on the screen door. Opening it, she hollered, "Hey, it's me."

"Good morning," he said with a chipper and spry tone.

Maddy rubbed her hands together. "I'm ready for my first lesson."

"First?" He cocked his head to the left.

"If it goes well, maybe you'd want to teach me something else. Cooking…canning. That sort of thing." She could feel her face turn warm.

"I have a few tricks up my sleeve I'd be happy to share. So, as you can see, I have everything out for us. Frozen berries, spices, honey, and jars. What we do first is add water to the pan then the berries and spices. Bring to a boil, simmer, and reduce the liquid to about half. We then take this potato masher and mash the berries. After that, we'll strain the juice into this large bowl. After that, we'll add the honey, make sure it's all mixed up good and then pour into these four mason jars. That's it. Pretty easy, right?"

"Sounds fairly easy." She moved to the sink and picked up the pot. "How much water?"

"Three and a half cups," he said, standing back watching.

She measured the water and dumped it into the pan. She casually turned toward him.

"Add the berries and spices," he said, coaching her along.

As they watched the pot boil, they sipped on freshly brewed coffee.

"Now we simmer and let the juice reduce," he said, putting the lid on.

She crossed her arms and rocked back on her heels. "So what do we do while we wait?"

He tapped his chin with his finger. "We could play cards. Do you like to play?"

"I haven't played cards in forever," she said.

"I play a lot of solitaire." He moved to the other room, pulling out a drawer and retrieving a deck. He held them up.

"I know gin rummy and a few poker games. That's about it."

"Gin rummy it is." He slid a chair out and motioned for her to sit.

"Don't let me ruin my first batch ever of elderberry syrup," she said teasingly.

"Don't worry. I'll keep a watchful eye on it."

His soft laugh made her feel comfortable, like a favorite pair of slippers.

After a hand of cards, the next step in syrup making took place.

She picked up the potato masher and began to mash.

"Here, let me help." His fingers touched hers as he took hold of the utensil. A wave of electricity bolted through her. Her bottom lip trembled. "Like this," he said, applying pressure to the berries, squishing all the juice out of them.

She drew in her bottom lip and swallowed. Her mouth was dry, and she desperately needed water.

"Thirsty," she squeaked out. "I need some water." She let go of the masher and stepped back, abundantly aware of how he made her feel, and concerned that she wanted to act on it.

"In the fridge," he said, motioning with his head.

She poured a glass of water and gulped it down. Trying to steady her nerves and put aside the deep-rooted feeling that sneaked up on her, she watched him as he finished mashing the berries. Twisting and plunging the utensil into the large stainless steel pot, his rigid and strong farm hands were hard at work. She bit down on her bottom lip.

"Listen, I just remembered I need to do something."

"But we're not finished. We still need to strain the berries and put them in jars."

"Can you finish that part for me. I'm sorry. I have to go. Fluffy. Come on, boy," she said, moving out of the space that was taking her breath away.

He dropped the masher and stepped toward her. "What's wrong, Maddy?"

"I don't know," she stuttered.

"Do I make you feel uncomfortable?"

"No," she said, not making eye contact with him.

He tilted her chin upward with his finger. "Then what?"

Her knees wobbled and started to bend. "I feel almost too comfortable around you," she said, straightening her posture while smoothing down her shirt.

"I'm glad you do. I know I feel at ease with you too," he said, inching his way closer.

Rubbing the back of her neck, she flashed him a sly grin. "I just got out of a bad relationship. You've recently lost your wife. It's probably too soon for either of us."

"Maybe. But maybe not. But that's not for us to decide right now. We were just making elderberry syrup." He placed his hands on her arms and smiled.

She laughed. "You do know how to make me laugh and make things seem right."

"Can we finish now?" He turned his head toward the berry concoction.

"Yes. Of course."

They worked alongside each other the rest of the time, laughing, talking, and trying the syrup for taste purposes. Maddy felt more relaxed, and even though there were moments of something between them, they both let it go, enjoying their time together.

"Those two jars will last a long time in the fridge. Just keep the lids on tight," he said as he walked her out.

She hugged her elderberry syrup as if it were a child. "I plan to take a teaspoon every day."

"Next time you come over we'll make pasta sauce."

She widened her eyes. His sauce was delicious. "Sounds great."

"In fact, I looked at those vines yesterday. They are just hanging with fruit."

She moved off the porch and started to head home. She suddenly stopped and whirled around. "Listen, John. Do you want to have dinner together?"

"Sure. When?" His answer came quick.

"Tonight?" She shrugged her shoulders, then let them drop.

"I have a pot of butternut squash soup simmering on the stove. Some crusted bread and soup, if you'd like to have dinner here."

"That sounds lovely."

"Come over in an hour or so."

Biting down a smile, Maddy whispered, "See you then."

SHE BRUSHED her hair and tossed it back behind her ears, putting on a black headband. She combed down a few bangs. Studying her image in the mirror, she nodded her approval. She rummaged through the small wooden box that held a few pairs of earrings, settling on some large silver hoops. Spritzing on a light floral cologne, she waved her hand in front of herself, letting the aroma waft around her.

Fluffy was excited about going with her. He was always up for a little nestling with his favorite black miniature poodle.

The main door was wide open. She peered into the black mesh netting of the screen door. A soft glow from the lights, along with a sweet, earthy smell coming from the kitchen, led her inside. She sniffed. Something besides soup was simmering on the stove. She wrinkled her nose.

"Hello. Hello," she called.

No answer.

"John. It's me. Maddy. We're here. Fluffy and me."

Nothing.

She walked into the kitchen. The simmering pot of soup was boiled over, burning onto the stove. She quickly turned off the burner. She sniffed. Burnt bread. She tossed open the oven. Smoke was coming from a foil packet. She searched for oven mitts. She pulled out the burning bread and threw it into the sink, then turned the water on it.

"Sheba," she called out.

Fluffy sniffed around the room.

"Where's John and your buddy Sheba?" She pushed out her lip. Moving around the adjacent sitting room near the kitchen, she thought about where to go next. A loud bang from another room startled her. Fluffy let out a bark.

"John?"

She heard a grunt. With her heart racing a mile a minute, she jumped into action and ran toward the sound. When she entered the room, her jaw dropped, and she gasped. John was lying on the floor with blood coming from his head.

She rushed to his side. Slipping her hand under his neck, she lifted his head slightly. His eyes were closed, but he was conscious. A moaning sound escaped his mouth.

"John. What happened?" She looked around for something to put on his wound.

He grunted.

She gently rested his head back on the hardwood floor. She moved to the adjacent bathroom and pulled a towel down from the bar and ran back to him.

"I need to call 911." She took out her cell and called while blotting his head with the towel.

In a matter of ten minutes, two men rushed into the house, carrying a black medical bag.

"Move away, ma'am."

Maddy did as she was instructed to, taking Fluffy outside.

When another man ran in with a stretcher, she really got nervous.

After a few minutes, they came out of the house, carrying John on the stretcher. He was awake but looked confused.

"Is he going to be alright?"

"He's got a nasty bump on his head. Probably a concussion. We're taking him to the hospital for observation."

"Sheba," he called out as they put him in the ambulance.

She rushed to the edge of the emergency vehicle. "I can't find her. Where did she go?"

"Under the bed. Look under the bed," he said.

"Please, wait. Let me find his dog," she said, pushing back from the ambulance. She ran inside to the bedroom where she had found John. She dropped to her knees and lifted the bed skirt, peering underneath. Little beady eyes followed by a low growl made her pull back for a second.

"Sheba. It's me, baby girl. Come on out." Maddy extended her hand.

Sheba inched her way to Maddy's hand.

"Come on, baby girl. It's okay."

Sheba licked her hand then crawled all the way out. Maddy picked her up and rushed outside, hoping the ambulance had not left.

She held up the dog in her arms, yelling, "She's here, John, she's here."

He lifted his head at the same time the crew closed the doors. But she was sure he saw her before the doors closed.

"He'll be at Memorial Hospital," the one crew member said.

They jumped into the cab and sped off, leaving Maddy holding Sheba and Fluffy sitting by her feet.

The three of them eventually went back inside. She cleaned up the kitchen and salvaged what she could of the soup, helping herself to a bowl. She fed Sheba, and when it got dark, she let the rest of the pack inside to feed them. They looked worried that John wasn't there.

She buttoned up the house, leaving a few lights on for Hazel, Marcus, Scruffy, and Sheba, promising them she'd be back soon. She dropped Fluffy off at the loft then headed to the hospital. She had no idea when visiting hours were over, but she had a few questions for John.

He was sitting up in bed, eating gelatin.

"Why is it they always give patients green gelatin?"

"Hi. Everything okay with Sheba and the rest of the dogs?" He put down his plastic spoon.

"Everyone is fine. She was under the bed, scared to death. What happened?" She pulled up a chair closer to his bed.

"I heard a knock at the door. Thought it was you. I yelled come in. The next thing I know, I'm being shoved against the counter, and someone was making demands. I started to fight with them, but alas, I lost."

"What kind of demands?" she asked.

"Money, jewelry."

"What did they hit you with?"

"The lid to the pot. Coldcocked me with it, and all I saw was stars."

"So, you don't know who they were?"

"He. It was only one guy. His face was covered with a black ski mask."

"We have to tell the police, John."

"No, I don't want to do that."

"Why not?"

"Just let me handle it my way. I'm sorry. That came out wrong."

"John, what is it you're not telling me?"

CHAPTER 10

"It's hospital procedure. He must leave in a wheelchair," the head nurse said.

Maddy wheeled him to her parked van, letting the hospital staff help him inside. She'd left Fluffy home even with all his persistence, which included nonstop whining and barking, no matter how many treats she'd given him.

Watching in her side mirror, she pulled out slowly, making her way out of the hospital grounds and onto the main road taking them back to his place. She wasn't sure how to start the conversation. She knew how'd they left it, but where to begin?

"I gave Sheba extra loving. She was shaking like a leaf," she said.

"Thank you."

"And the other dogs knew something was up, but being the well-rounded pack that they are, they handled it quite well." She looked over at him once again.

"Thank you," he responded, his eyes remaining straight ahead.

She put her gaze back to the road and drove. Finally, the silence far more annoying than anything she or he could possibly say, she opened her mouth.

"I know you're hiding something. Why can't you tell me?"

"I will tell you, but not right now."

After about twenty minutes or so, they pulled into the farm. She drove him right up to the front porch. Hazel, Scruffy, and Marcus all leaped off the porch and ran to him, wagging their tails and barking happy salutations.

He rubbed them all on the head and back. "Where's Sheba? Inside?"

"Yes. Her highness is perched on her favorite pillow, awaiting her king." She laughed.

He shot her a jaunty look, causing her to step back.

"Just kidding. You know I think she's a cutie. And Fluffy, well, they're best buds."

"I'm sorry. Just a bit on edge is all." He climbed the few steps up the porch.

"Can I get you anything? Help you settle in before I

go to my place?" She followed close behind him into the house.

"No, we'll be alright. Thanks for taking care of my dogs. They're all the family I have."

That seemed like an odd thing for him to say. He never struck her as the woe is me sort of fellow. No, quite the opposite. He emitted strength through every aspect of his being. By the way he held his body, the way he steadied his voice, calm and collected, the way he looked at her…

"You never told me that before." She fixed her gaze on him.

"It's true. I guess I don't like to discuss it."

"You said the Amish folks were there for you when Sarah passed. I see them come around now too. They're like your family, huh?" She tried to urge him to tell her more.

"You could say that. But when it's said and done, only a dog is man's true best friend."

She tipped her chin. She believed that, too, sort of. But she did have her parents, and they were supportive in their own little warped way.

"I hope you see me as a friend. I'm trying my best to show you I care."

He stepped forward. "I do see that. And I appreciate it."

"I know it's probably none of my business, but do your parents live around here?"

"I'm tired. Doctor said I should rest. Please come back another time." He placed his hand on her arm and guided her toward the door.

She shook off his hand. "Okay, I got the message. You're a strange guy. First, you act as if maybe we could be friends, maybe more than friends. Then, you usher me out as if you never want to see me again. Talk about mixed messages." She moved to the door. "Don't worry. I won't intrude on you any longer. In fact, consider this my notice."

"Notice?" he said.

"I'm leaving the loft. At the end of this month."

"Maddy," he said.

She rushed to the screen door, throwing it open and letting it bang shut.

He trailed off after her, insisting she'd taken it wrong.

"Don't," she said, pushing his hand away.

"I'm sorry. I just don't know what to do...or say anymore."

"You've said quite enough, John. I get the message. You want to be alone. I'm going to honor your wish." She moved down the stairs quickly, jumped into her van, and sped off, tears rolling down her cheeks. Once parked, she grabbed the steering wheel and dropped her head onto her hands, crying.

SHE KNEW how to avoid him. She made sure Fluffy did his business before he got up, although once she caught him staring at her through the curtains, creeping her out some. The pounding of hammers as the festival came together was annoying, especially since she had to avoid it, but she did her best by wearing earbuds while listening to music and drowning out the noise and laughter. The laughter was the hardest. Everyone was having a good time, or so it seemed, and she and Fluffy were locked in the loft, like prisoners counting down the days until release.

She left early each morning to attend to her grooming appointments, leaving an hour or two before schedule just to avoid him. But avoiding him was hard. After four days of giving him his space, asked indirectly or not, Maddy made the mistake of taking Fluffy for a walk. She hoped the construction crew was gone, and he should be in his house eating his homemade meals. But nope. That wasn't to be. She walked right smack into him. He'd been in the corn maze and popped out at the end, scaring them both. She shrieked, Fluffy yelped, then put his tail between his legs, and John palmed his chest and apologized for scaring them half to death.

"Jeez, John! You scared the *you know what* out of us."

"I'm sorry. I didn't expect anyone to be here. I was just checking out the maze. The kids are going to love it."

His twinkling eyes melted her heart. But she stiffened her back and shrugged off the weakness.

"Yes, I see you're about ready." She nodded to the wooden stands dotting the farm.

"In a few more days, this place will be full of youngsters screaming, having fun, running around like banshees."

"Good for them. Fall is a great time for having fun," she said, still holding her snide tone.

"Listen, Maddy. I need to apologize."

"You already did that. We jump at the slightest noise, don't we Fluffy." She reached over and ran her hand down his back.

"No, not for scaring you, but for not being truthful with you. I know we don't know each other that well, but you're right, we did hit it off. I wanted to let you in, I really did. But I got scared."

She moved toward him, feeling her smugness drift away. "I get scared, too, sometimes," she whispered.

"Come over to the house. I'll put on the coffee."

"Are you sure?" She lifted her brows.

"I've never been surer."

It felt odd to be back inside the house, but once Fluffy and Sheba pranced around and sniffed each other, all was well. He set the cup of coffee in front of her.

"I made chocolate chip cookies."

"Of course, you did. That's what any man does who lives by themselves, was just released from the hospital, and who has a dairy farm." She shrugged.

He scooped a few onto a plate and slid it on the table.

"I bake to help me cope."

"I eat to help me cope." She laughed.

They talked well into the night. He warmed up butternut soup and bread when they realized neither of them had eaten dinner. When she was standing next to him, drying the dishes as he washed, he dropped the bomb on her. The one she knew was there, but nevertheless, when it hit her, it hit her hard. Still reeling from the announcement, her head dizzy with doubt, questions and more questions, she moved to a chair. Holding the back, she steadied her wobbly legs.

"Are you alright? I know it's a lot to digest."

She slid her hand down the chair back and dropped her body onto the chair.

"It's been a burden hiding it."

"I bet."

"I wish you'd say something. Anything." His eyes grew misty.

"I suspected something. But I didn't think anything this large. I mean…you were…are…Amish?"

"Well, not really, but sort of. My mom grew up near here. My dad was an Englisher. She met him during Rumspringa. He was the good-looking farm boy, and she was the Amish teen sowing her wild oats, I guess you could say."

"It's kind of romantic to think that a runaway teen from a tight-knit community such as this could fall in love with a commoner," she said.

"It happens. Not a lot, but it does. So yeah, they got together, and when Rumspringa was over with, she went back home, and he went back to bailing hay, feeding cows and such. Right here on this property."

"Wow. This sounds like a novel or something." She widened her eyes as she listened. She was all ears too. This explained so much about his mysterious ways. Sitting on the edge of her seat, she set her clasped hands on the table, keeping her eyes focused on John as he recapped his parent's romantic escapade.

"Mom was sixteen years old. Dad was eighteen. They told me they immediately hit it off. Two young people from totally different cultures. The one thing they did have in common is my grandparents came over from Germany. Mom spoke Pennsylvania Dutch. I assume they thought that was enough to keep them together."

Maddy sighed. "Keep going."

"Well, one thing led to another, and when she went back home, he was heartbroken. He became brazen and started hanging around her family's farm. Her dad was not too happy about that, either."

"I bet. Some of those Amish men look mean. It's their serious face."

"So anyway, they started sneaking around. Her parents were pressuring her to marry some guy they picked out for her, and when she felt cornered, she bolted."

"And then they disowned her, right?" Maddy crossed her legs, her foot juddering in rapid sequence.

"Sort of. You read about the kids who go off on Rumspringa and never return, becoming ostracized by the community and all of that. And don't get me wrong, Mom and Dad said they'd be alone if it weren't for my grandparents. But Mom told me on occasion that after I was born, that her mom would take the buggy and sneak over to see me and her. Her dad never came. But Mom made her choice, and she said she didn't have a single regret."

"Did you believe her? That she didn't have any regrets?"

"I did. They were in love. Working the land together, raising me and my sister, Mary, and taking care of the farm."

"That's where you learned to cook, wasn't it? From your mom," Maddy asked.

"Yep. She was a wonderful cook. Everything from scratch."

Maddy looked around the house. It was furnished starkly. She just thought it was because he was a bachelor.

"What happened to your folks...and your grand-parents?"

"My grandfather died when I was a baby. I didn't know him. My grandmother died a few years back. She was never the same after..."

Maddy's jaw dropped. This was bad. She could tell. His tone dropped, his eyes misted, he was about to lay it on her again. She gulped. "What happened?"

"Mom and Dad were on their way into town to get some supplies. They were driving the old pickup when it stalled on the side of the road. Dad was under the hood, tinkering. Mom got impatient and opened up her door to go see what he was up to. A big semi-truck was barreling down the road and hit the door, killing Mom and Dad instantly."

"Oh, John. That's horrific." She reached out and touched his hand. "What did her parents do? Anything?"

"Her family came to the house a couple of times. But it was very strange. They talked in hushed tones with my grandmother and then would pray over us. I think my grandmother got tired of them and asked them to not come back."

"The buggies I see here sometimes…friends or relatives?"

"Both. The man you see here most often is my uncle. If that's what you want to call him. My mother's brother. He comes occasionally, but it's odd because he doesn't ask me anything about me. He just talks about farming, and says a prayer and leaves."

"That is odd," Maddy said.

"But I let him in, because why not? They can't do anything to me."

Maddy's jaw dropped, and she gasped. "Wait! The break-in the other day. Could this be connected somehow?"

"No," he said adamantly, shaking his head. "They'd never hurt me. They won't embrace me, but I don't believe they'd want me harmed."

"Well, what was that about then?" Maddy narrowed her gaze.

"I have a suspicion that it was the son of a local farmer. He wants me to sell some of my land, and I won't. We've been arguing about it since my grandmother passed. He thinks just because she's gone, I'll cave. But I won't."

"Why would he think that?" Maddy tilted her head.

He leaned back and crossed his arms, letting out a long-winded breath.

"Is there more?" Maddy raised her brows.

"Yeah, a little. See, I'm just full of surprises, aren't I?" He chuckled.

"Just a little. What now?" Maddy moved forward, picking up her cooled coffee.

"Let me heat that up for you," he said, jumping up and taking the cup out of her hand.

She watched as he pressed the start button on the microwave.

"I bet your mom never used a microwave," Maddy said.

"Nope. I got this just a few years ago." He crossed over to the table and set the steaming mug in front of her.

"Thank you. So, please continue." The corners of her mouth drew up in a smile.

"My dad's brother and his family live about fifteen miles from here. They never accepted Mom. I don't know why because she was the sweetest woman on earth. Her only sin was she married the man she loved and left a community that couldn't understand her choice."

A tear bobbled on Maddy's bottom lid. "This story is so moving. I'm going to cry."

He patted her hand, but then instead of lifting his away, he left it there. The warmth of his body temperature radiated through her, making her pulse race and her throat go dry. John was so kind it even resonated through his touch. She blinked back the emotions and tried to refrain from falling apart. But it was hard. His vulnerability made her want him even more.

"The guy that coldcocked me in the head…my cousin." His matter-of-fact nod astonished her.

"You accept that your cousin, your flesh and blood would harm you? You're alright with that?" Maddy knitted her brows together.

"Not alright with it, but what am I going to do? I'm not selling them any of the land. So, who is really winning here?"

"I think it's sad that your parents are gone, your grandmother is gone, and you have relatives down the road who are being rotten."

"It is what it is."

Maddy gazed at her watch. "Oh my! It's after midnight. I should be going."

"I'm sorry. I've talked your ear off. Let me walk you guys home."

The cool night air hit her in the face. It was refreshing after hearing all the horrid details of his life. She looked over at him as he held her arm, leading her around the corn in the still of the night. He didn't really look like a guy who'd been through the kind of life he'd told her about. Maybe he was strong enough to handle it all. They stopped in front of the barn door.

"Can I go up and make sure everything is okay? I just don't want any surprises awaiting you."

"You're scaring me, John." She laced her arm with his as they entered the barn. Fluffy ran up the stairs and waited on the small stoop for them.

"I guess I should start locking my door." She pushed it open.

He held up a hand for her to wait. Fluffy couldn't read hand signals, so he ducked between his legs and went straight inside.

"Coast is clear," he said, waving her to come in.

"Thanks for walking me home. Now I'm going to be worried that you get home safely." She stepped closer toward him.

"Don't worry about me," he said.

His low tone and his steady eyes drew her in, and she found herself moving in closer. "But I will. Call me after you get home."

His gaze bobbled around her face, flitting to every corner. She wondered what he was thinking as he canvased her features.

Stepping closer, he slipped his arms around her waist, pulling her next to him. Her stomach rolled and pitched, and a light-headedness came on, making her feel giddy.

"Maddy, from the first day we met, I knew you were special. I know I've kept some secrets from you, but please let me make it up to you. From here on out, no more secrets."

The quickening of her breath, along with her racing heart, let her know something big was about to happen. She leaned back, loving the feel of security in his strong arms, and planting her feet, she posed for the kiss.

Slowly, he slid his hand behind her head, guiding her to move closer. Making a gentle stroke on her cheek with his thumb, he looked deeply into her eyes.

"Are you sure this is alright with you?" His sultry voice sent shivers down her spine.

An unhurried nod was all she was capable of providing at this point.

"I don't want you to ever think I make out with all of my tenants. I'll have you know, the last one to rent the loft was a fifty-year-old man. Not my type." He held her back, swaying her lightly, a coy smile on his face.

"I wasn't worried about that. I'm a big girl." She reached up and played with the ends of his hair, aware of her own sultriness being exposed.

"Well, in that case, what are we waiting for?"

Lowering his head, he moved forward, their lips touching.

She rolled her head slightly and met his warm, inviting mouth.

It was a much longer kiss than she'd expected, but one she definitely didn't want to end. Sliding her hands around the base of his neck, she locked her fingers and moved closer to him while deepening the kiss.

Blank page?

CHAPTER 11

Sitting on the edge of her bed, Maddy replayed the evening's events. She touched her mouth, recalling the magical kiss. Still in a fog over everything that had transpired, she was sure sleep would not come easy.

Maddy had hoped there was some deep, dark secret John wasn't telling her, and if she were to be completely honest, just a tad of her wished he had something worth a scandal at least. She laughed out loud at her ridiculous thought.

She undressed and crawled into bed. Every time she closed her eyes, she'd see him as he leaned in for their good-night kiss. She didn't deserve to be happy. Ryan saw to that. She turned on her side. The moonlight peeked in through her one and only window. Rolling onto her back, she stared at the ceiling for a while. Counting the wood beams like sheep, she soon fell asleep.

TALK ABOUT AWKWARD. What would she say to him? She pondered over her morning coffee. Maybe he'd feel some regret for letting it go as far as it did. Far? *A kiss is not exactly far, Maddy.* But then there was the issue of her own heavy baggage. The one she carried all the way to Lancaster. The one she trusted she could dump along the road side, setting her free, but alas, that wasn't to happen. She didn't have what it took to be someone's better half. What was it Ryan told her? She wasn't even good enough to scrape his boots on. She hugged her arms and shivered. Why on earth did she stay around so long?

She rinsed out her cup, leashed up Fluffy, and with squared shoulders, faced the day. Maddy secretly hoped she'd run into John, but didn't know exactly what she'd say.

There he was. Waiting for her. Pacing back and forth along the house, his hands deep in his pockets, his scowl told her he was deep in thought.

She rolled down her window and greeted him.

He walked up to the window, resting his arm on the ledge. His dreamy eyes talked to her. She lightly licked her dry mouth.

"Good morning," she squeaked out in a raspy tone.

"I've been waiting for you."

"Oh?"

"I want to apologize for coming on so strong with you last night. I don't know what came over me."

"Came on so strong? You mean the kiss?"

"Yes, that."

She smiled at his flushed complexion. He really was bothered by his advances. A real gentleman.

"No worries. It was just a kiss."

"Just a kiss? Is that how you saw it?" He peered at her through half-closed lids.

"Well, that's all it was, right?" she asked, serving the ball back to him.

"For me, it was magical. Can a guy say that without any labels being put on him?"

"Sure. I'd never judge." She let out a small laugh.

"I was hoping it felt magical to you as well." His eyes focused on her, not blinking a lash.

"Listen, John. You know I like you. We hit it off great. But I'm not looking for a relationship. In fact, I'm considering moving back to Philly. But right now, I have a few appointments to get to. We'll talk later." She quickly rolled up the window and accelerated the van forward.

With flushed cheeks and a look of sheer frustration, he jumped back. She drove off, leaving him standing in the driveway. She peered up once in the rearview mirror and saw him run his hand through his hair, then shaking his head, he turned and walked back to where he came from.

Thumping her head back onto the headrest, she groaned loudly. "Why?" Then she sped off to Mrs. Mitchell's house. A certain three-legged terrier named Cocoa was waiting for her bath.

AFTER A FULL DAY OF APPOINTMENTS, Maddy found something else to keep her and Fluffy busy. She was not in any hurry to get home to face John. She stopped into the local market and chatted with some of the Amish women. She found them interesting, although they didn't say a whole lot. She wondered about John's mother and how she must have been at the age of sixteen. There was a young woman probably about that age, dressed in traditional clothing, stocking shelves. When Maddy thought of sixteen-year-old girls in other societies, she pictured them with cell phones, wearing skimpy clothing, and having boyfriends. *I guess maybe that's what John's mom wanted too?* Although it was probably more about falling in love with John's dad than anything else.

After the market, she stopped into an Amish furniture store. The workmanship of the pieces was excellent. Dovetailed corners, smooth finishes, and natural stains, she ran her hand over a bookcase. She noticed immediately she didn't get bombarded with salesmen. Nope, the Amish folks let you look without getting pestered. She bid them goodbye when she noticed the store hours, and that she was keeping them late.

"Well, Fluffy, I guess we'll head home. I'm hungry, and you must be too."

JOHN BOLTED out the screen door and stood in front of her van, making her slam on her brakes. Throwing her hands up in the air, she screamed at him through the windshield.

He ran over to her side.

Rolling down the window, she glared at him. "I could have killed you. What is wrong with you?"

"I think we have some unfinished business," he said firmly.

She had to admit it. She liked this new side of him. Although she also adored the smooth-talking, quiet John. The nice boy or the bad boy. Choices.

"We don't have any unfinished business, John," she said pointedly

She could see the strain on his face. The clenched jaw, the narrowed eyes. What happened to her blushing John?

"Let me get Fluffy inside and fix his dinner. We've had a long day. I'm starving too. I'll come over in a while."

"I have some food in the oven. Been keeping it warm. Please. Have dinner with me."

She blinked. Nice boy was back.

"YOU DIDN'T BRING Fluffy with you?" He carried his gaze back up to her.

"He's exhausted. As I am. But I never turn away a free home-cooked meal."

"Sit down. I'll dish it up."

"Something smells delicious. What is it?"

"Chicken and rice casserole."

Maddy looked around the sparse room. It really could use a woman's touch. But it had one at one time.

Guess John's mother never cared for materialistic things.

"I can't help but notice the quaint furnishings of your house. Was this the way your mom and dad lived too?"

He pulled out the casserole dish and set it on a trivet.

Realizing he'd not answered her, she tried again.

"Sometimes, less is better. I'm sure your mom didn't have much growing up, so she didn't know what she was missing."

"True. She left when she was a teen. Dad didn't have a lot to offer her in the way of things. They had the ranch, and they worked hard every day of their lives."

He set a plate in front of her, the steam rising up and tickling her senses with spices, making her tummy growl.

She dug into the dish, blowing on it once, then tasting it. "Yummy."

"Can we talk while we eat?" he asked.

"Sure."

"I felt something last night. Are you going to tell me you didn't?"

She dropped the fork next to her plate and made eye contact with him.

"If you're asking me if I felt anything with the kiss, yes, I did. Am I asking you to be anything more to me than what we have now? No."

"I don't just go around kissing women, or inviting them to my house and fixing them dinner. That's just not me, Maddy."

"I know, John. I get it. You're a nice guy. I'm a girl from the big bad city who drives around in a dog grooming van."

He shoved his chair back and stood. "That's just plain crazy talk. I may be a nice guy, but you're a nice girl too. I wouldn't have you in my house if I thought any differently." He pulled her up out of the chair, taking her by surprise.

"John. Don't."

"Don't because you don't want me to, or don't because it's not right?" He slipped his hand around her waist, holding her steady.

Lowering her gaze, she studied the floor.

"Maddy," he said, lifting her chin.

"I may be a country farmer, but I know when I feel something deep in the pit of my stomach. You make me feel so alive inside. I can't stop thinking about you."

"John, I've been thinking about moving back to the city."

He dropped his hold and stepped back.

"I'm getting tired of the routine here. I needed the distraction, but now I'm longing to go home. I've enjoyed our friendship and hope you won't be angry with me."

He poked his tongue against his cheek and exhaled, followed by quick, jerky movements.

Maddy reached out and touched his arm. "John, please—"

He shook her off and moved to the sink. "Go. You've made it clear. You never had any intentions of sticking around. It's all been a game to you. I don't have time for games or drama."

She walked out of the kitchen, not saying another word. When she got inside the loft, she began to pack up her few belongings as Fluffy watched. She'd already canceled all her upcoming appointments, letting them know she was leaving, maybe permanently out of the area. She'd already decided that she wasn't good enough for John. He deserved so much more than she could ever offer him. At least that was what Ryan always told her. She wasn't worthy of any man. Her only companion would be her dumb dog. His words, not hers. Sniffling back tears, she finished packing, made sure the loft was clean, and she and Fluffy headed back to Philly.

CHAPTER 12

Her parents were cool about letting her and Fluffy stay until she decided what she would do in terms of housing. Having her job go with her wherever she went was clever, but going back to Philly also drummed up some bad vibes for Maddy, and she wasn't sure if coming back was in her and Fluffy's best interest.

"What are your plans, dear?"

Maddy cringed when she saw her mom's doe-like eyes study her. It often meant a deeper discussion was about to be had, and she wasn't in the mood for it.

"Mom, I just got here. Give me a few days to figure it out."

"Honey, I didn't mean anything by it. I was just curious." She wiped her hand on the apron tied around her waist.

Maddy watched as her mom pulled out fresh-baked biscuits and wondered why she never took to cooking or baking.

"I'll probably get my business going again as a start." Maddy drew a sip of the coffee as she watched her mom lift the golden-brown balls onto a plate, the smell wafting over to her, making her tummy growl.

"That's a good idea."

"Then after I get some business going, I'll look for an apartment."

"You're welcome to stay in the basement as long as you need."

The basement wasn't really a basement, except it was located on the bottom floor. With paneled walls, a soft comfy sofa, a bedroom, and a bath, the only thing it was missing was a kitchen, and with her mom being Suzy homemaker food would never be an issue.

"I know, but I'll eventually want my own space. Thanks, though."

"Dad and I are going to go see a movie. Interested?" Her mom's smile lit up the room.

"No, you two go and enjoy. Fluffy and I are going to hang out here. I'll take him for a long walk, and start on my new business plan."

"Okay, if you're sure. We were going to grab a bite of dinner afterward."

For a brief moment, Maddy worried about dinner. That was ridiculous. A woman who lived on ramen was worried about that? Her mom's cooking had that effect.

"I'll grab a sandwich at the corner deli. Don't worry about me."

Maddy watched as her mom untied her apron and looped it over the hook on the back of the pantry door.

"Those biscuits," Maddy said, tipping her head toward them.

"Help yourself. There's butter, jam, and honey too." She winked.

Maddy slid out her chair and bounced over to the counter where the biscuits were. She opened the folded cloth and took one out. Looking over her shoulder, she laughed.

"Who am I fooling. This is a two-biscuit day." She went in for another.

WITH BOTH OF her parents gone for most of the afternoon, the house was oddly quiet. She walked Fluffy over to the park and let him play with some other dogs.

While sitting on a bench watching the dogs romp inside the fenced dog park, her phone rang.

She stared at the incoming number, and just before it went to voice mail, answered it.

"How are you?" John asked.

"I'm good. You?"

"Good. Glad you made it back to Philly safely. I was hoping you'd let me know."

"Why would I do that?" she asked.

"Oh, I don't know. Because maybe we are friends?" John said, his tone holding a light sarcasm.

She felt bad for sounding like such a spoiled child. They were friends. But it just wasn't fair to him for her to stick around, wishing for more but realizing they'd never be more.

"I'm sorry. You're right. We are friends. But I'm sort of trying to figure things out right now."

"Did I mess things up by telling you the truth about me?" he asked.

"No, it wasn't that. I appreciated that you decided to confide in me. I have my own baggage. I can't let anyone get close to me."

"I can understand that, with what you dealt with because of your last boyfriend. I'm kind of shy too. But I guess you knew that already."

His shyness was what attracted her to him. His boy

next door charm combined with his wickedly good looks, strong arms, and bold features; it was enough to make any woman swoon. He didn't know he had the *it* factor.

"I decided to stay with my parents for a bit."

"Well, I'm not going to rent the loft out again. It'll be here if you change your mind."

"That's not necessary, John. You shouldn't keep it vacant for me. I probably will not come back."

"I'd rather keep it available. And as long as you say probably not coming back, I have a chance to see you again. I'd like to see you again, Maddy."

"I don't know, John. I'm a mess right now."

"I told you the truth about me because I wanted to let you in. It wasn't easy for me. Don't let it be in vain."

She drew in her bottom lip and paused before answering. She liked him from their first meeting. She was attracted to him, and he seemed to like her. And he liked dogs. Perhaps she'd run off too quickly. Didn't give him enough of a chance.

"I know it wasn't easy for you to tell me all of that. And likewise, I confided in you. I didn't realize just how badly Ryan scarred me until I recounted our history with you. I stayed with him for too long. But to answer you, I'd like to see you again too. Maybe I can come for a weekend and visit."

"The festival is kicking off. I'd love for you to come back and see it. You can stay in the loft."

"I'll think about it," she said.

When they hung up from their conversation, she sat dazed for a few moments. The dogs were galloping around the fenced area, barking and playing. John left her feeling even more confused, but a flash of warmth traveling through her veins told her it might not be such a bad thing.

"BUT YOU JUST GOT HERE," Emma Jean said.

"I know, but I've got some unfinished business in Lancaster."

"Oh?" Emma Jean tilted her head.

"I met this guy."

Emma Jean threw her hands up in the air.

"A nice guy. A farmer who is soft-spoken, kind, and the total opposite of Ryan."

"How can you be sure?" her mother asked, taking a seat at the table.

"I think I just feel it here," she said, tapping her chest.

"Well, they say the heart knows best." Emma rested her hand on top of hers.

"He's so different from Ryan. Living off the land,

loves animals, gives back to his community, has a little baggage of his own, but I think we can work through all of that."

"What sort of baggage?" her mom asked.

"He's been married before."

Her mother gasped. "A divorcee?"

"Mom, no! His wife died. Of cancer."

"Oh, I'm so sorry for jumping to conclusions. He's so young to be a widower."

"There's more."

Emma Jean leaned back.

"His mother was Amish."

"Was?"

"It's a long story, but she left the community to marry John's dad."

"His deceased wife?"

"He hasn't talked about her much except to tell me how much he loved her. But when I asked what her name was, he said, Sarah."

"And you think there might be more to the story? Like mother, like son?"

"Maybe. But that's why I have to go back. I already told him about Ryan and how he has scarred me from believing I'm worthy of anyone. I need to make sure he's told me everything so we can figure it all out."

"I'm proud of you, dear. You've never been bashful

about going after what you want. I remember when you told us your crazy idea of a mobile grooming business. Now, look at you. You're making a living doing it."

"Yes, but I'm getting a bit tired of grooming. I think I have another calling. Thanks for understanding, Mom. It really means a lot to me. I love you and Dad, and I'm so happy you always have my back."

"Of course, we do. That's what families are for."

"Not always. John has a crazy cousin who is trying to hurt him. Literally."

"That's not good," Emma Jean said.

"I'm leaving in the morning. I'll let you know how things go."

"Hon," Emma Jean said.

Maddy cocked her head.

"I'm hoping the best for you. You do deserve happiness, and Ryan can't decide that for you. He's a jerk, a nobody, and you must erase him from your mind. It was one experience in your long life of many. Don't let him define you."

Maddy pushed back her chair and ran over to her mother, resting her head on her mom's shoulder. "See, this is why I love you so much."

Emma Jean reached up and patted her daughter's arm. "Family. We're in it for the long haul. The good, the bad, and the ugly." She let out a chuckle.

For once in her life, Maddy was happy she only had a few belongings that mostly fit in a couple of boxes and her large duffel bag. But if she were to be completely honest, she longed to put down some roots, and maybe even be the owner of some things. Although she'd never coveted a lot. It just wasn't in her DNA, but having a few prized possessions besides her van would be nice.

The drive back to Lancaster was uneventful. She made sure she didn't speed, and she didn't stop at any stores where she might encounter crazy folks. She drove straight to the dairy farm.

When she pulled in, her jaw fell open in wonderment. What a transformation the area took on. All the booths were built and lined up, the maze was finished, and the smell of homemade food wafted through her windows.

She drove slowly, paying attention not to kick up a lot of dust and parked around the back where she'd always parked. She and Fluffy made their way to John's house. She knocked twice. When there was no answer, she decided to check out the festival. People were gathering, but it was still kind of low-key. A few kids ran around the maze, and some were just moseying along, looking at the sights. In the distance, a hay wagon was hitched, and people were climbing up into the wagon for a ride.

"Hey stranger," a soft voice said behind her.

She twirled around and met his cool eyes.

"Hey," she said, tossing a wave and smiling. "I went to your door but no answer," she said.

"That's because I'm out here, supervising." He dipped his hands in his pockets and rocked back on his heels.

"I see. Not a huge crowd yet," she said, looking out toward the festival.

"We just opened about twenty minutes ago. You're just in time."

"Good," she said, not sure what else to add.

"Can I buy you lunch?"

"That sounds good. I'm starving."

"Follow me," he said, taking her hand.

She pulled Fluffy along as he tugged her to a booth.

They stood in front of the booth and looked it over.

They took their sausages on a stick and found an empty bench.

"After this, I know where we can get homemade chocolate," he said.

"Chocolate. You know how to get to a girl's heart, don't you?"

He clasped her hand in his. "I might have a few ideas up my sleeve."

She tightened her fingers around his. "John, I feel we have so much to still try and figure out."

"We do. But we have lots of time. Rome wasn't built in a day, ya know." He gently bumped shoulders with her.

"True. I just want to get all the secrets out…so we can move forward."

"Secrets, or just stuff? There's a difference."

The way he studied her face made her squirm. "You've told me all of your secrets?"

"Yes. If you're asking me specifically about Sarah, I have a few things to share, but it's odd to tell another woman so much about the woman I loved." He hung his head.

"I know, John. I get it. I don't want you to tell me sacred things. That's between you and Sarah. But I just want to know you're not hiding anything from me. I told you, I'm damaged goods."

"You're not damaged goods. Stop saying that."

"I just know your mom left the community. I wonder if Sarah did too."

He blinked several times. His stiffened jaw told her she might have come across something sensitive.

"Her mother and father both left the community during Rumspringa. So even though she wasn't raised as Amish, there were always these reminders where they came from."

She nodded as she interpreted the new information. "What sort of reminders?"

"Their homes were furnished sparsely, they lived on the land, her mother made all their clothes, that sort of thing."

"Like you do?" she said.

"Well, the apple doesn't fall far from the tree." He flashed a wide grin.

"Any brothers or sisters?" Maddy asked.

"Four brothers."

"Where are they?"

"They live in Ohio. She wanted to leave the area, so she came out here. She still felt relaxed around the Amish even though her community shunned them. But here, they didn't really know anything, and we didn't share. The Amish folks here were a blessing to us during her illness."

"Does her family come here to visit?"

"When she left Ohio, she made Lancaster County her home. I hear from them from time to time. They live a simple life. Her brothers have come a couple of times."

"That's so sad. Two families split apart by distance, and by prejudices."

"I don't owe anyone anything, and I live by my own standards. I deserve to be happy, and so do you," he said, his tone steady and to the point.

"I agree with you, but my heart says one thing, and my head says something else."

"Time for chocolate then." He pulled her up by her hand.

Savoring the sweetness of the homemade chocolate and her elation of enjoying a gorgeous fall day with John, an invigorating feeling came over Maddy, making her swing her arms and hum quietly. The splendid array of colors surrounded them like a kaleidoscope with vivid reds, browns, oranges, and yellows, and the brisk, clean air put a bounce in their step as they made their way around the festival.

"Oh, look. Homemade apple butter," Maddy said, reaching for the jar with a gingham ribbon around the top.

"And peanut butter," John said, pointing to the other jars lined up.

After they sampled some of the items, Maddy couldn't decide.

"Get one of each. You can't go wrong with their preserves. It goes great with the peanut butter," John said.

They stopped at the cheese booth where they did more sampling, and John purchased a block of white cheddar. But when they stopped by the huge display of furniture and other items made of wood, Maddy was like a kid in a candy store. She sat in the Adirondack chairs, ran her hand along the smooth wood of the side tables, peeked inside the drawers of the dressers, and rocked the cradles.

"They do such beautiful work," she said, admiring a small table with three legs.

"They do. It's made to last and last."

"One of these days when I have a house of my own, I'd like to buy a few of these items. But right now, I'm in between places."

John took her hand in his and squeezed it gently. "It doesn't have to be that way, you know."

Her hands began to tingle, and a lightness in her limbs gave way to an overall feeling of weightlessness.

Taking deep, calming breaths, she considered how to reply.

Shaking her head softly, she said, "I know, John. I'm so confused right now."

The laughter from children nearby saved her from saying much more. Three Amish girls wearing dresses to their ankles and white kapps covering their heads ran past them, giggling. Maddy smiled at them as they ran past.

"They're having fun," she said, trying to stay away from any more sensitive subjects.

"They just came out of the maze," John said.

Maddy looked across the way and saw the corn maze. "Shall we try our luck at it?"

As they weaved their way around the corners, Maddy took in the earthy smells of the dirt pathways. She'd let her fingers rustle through the leaves and marvel at the warmth of the sunshine as it peeked through the four- and five-foot-tall stalks.

Children raced past them as they found their way out of the maze, while Maddy and John took a slower approach.

"I love to see the kids having so much fun," he said.

"Especially the little Amish girls," Maddy said.

"Why do you say that?" He stopped.

"Oh, I don't know. Maybe because I think they work hard and don't get to play and be kids." She shrugged.

John shook his head. "On the contrary. They do work hard, have chores to do, and all of that. The girls help their mothers and the boys work in the fields when they're old enough, but they have so much fun too. Their brothers and sisters are their best friends, so there is always someone to play with. And just like they make great furniture, they make even better toys. Wagons, pull toys, cradles for the baby dolls—"

"You mean the faceless dolls? They sort of creep me out," she said, cutting him off.

"You know why they are faceless, don't you?"

"No mirrors or something like that," Maddy said, starting to walk again.

He nodded, then reached for her hand.

Just as they laced fingers, a group of giggling kids came roaring through. They pulled up their locked hands, and the kids ran under their arms.

"It's getting a bit dangerous out here." John chuckled.

"John. I've been thinking a lot about giving up the mobile grooming business. I need something more challenging. I love the animals, but to tell you the truth, I'm getting bored."

"Perhaps go back to school and become a veterinarian?"

"I thought about that. I hate to see the fur babies suffering, though."

"You'd never let them suffer, Maddy. That's what a great vet understands. You'd be helping the ones you could, and for those you can't, you'd end their suffering."

They moved to the side to let a family walk by.

"Let's turn here," John said.

They walked along a bit further, turning here and there, going straight and turning some more.

"I think we're getting to the end. I can hear talk nearby."

"Or maybe you could work on the farm with me."

His words left her speechless.

"I could teach you how to drive a tractor, milk a cow, shear a sheep, feed the pigs. It's a full-time job and then some." He circled her thumb with his.

"And teach me how to can preserves and bake bread?" She raised her brows. "Make me into an Amish woman?"

"Maddy." He jerked her to a stop.

"I'm just kidding," she said.

"I'd never change you into something you are not. Remember, my mom ran away from that."

"It sounds lovely, really it does. I'm just a hippy in modern times anyway. I like things simple. However, I do love my electronic gadgets." The corners of her mouth drew up.

"I never cared much for them, but I'd never tell you to get rid of them."

"Good," she said, trying to figure out where exactly this was heading.

"You can stay in the loft, let me show you the ropes, and if you like it, you can stay on permanently."

"You sound as if you are interviewing for a hired hand." She knitted her brows.

"Haha, Maddy Pryor. I'm just merely suggesting you give me a chance. See if you have what it takes. Farming is hard work, and you city girls aren't used to getting your fingernails dirty."

"John Cooper, just you wait and see. This city girl used to be a major tomboy. I could shimmy up a tree before any of my guy friends, and I could wrap my legs around the limbs and swing back and forth upside down. Please. These hands have gotten pretty dirty in their time. You're on."

Leading her out of the maze, he said, "So, you'll head back to Philly and get your things?"

"Get my things? They're in the van."

He pulled her hand up to his mouth and kissed her knuckles as they locked gazes.

After finding their way out of the corn maze, they took a hayride. The horse-drawn wagon took them deep into the woods. The tall canopies of the trees barely let in any light, and as the day waned, the sun began to set, and a gray, ominous sky blew in. Someone in the wagon started telling ghost stories, and the children began to scream. Maddy and John cuddled near the back, listening to the tall tales of the headless horse rider. All of a sudden, the horses stopped, and the wagon master turned to address the group. The children held hands and held their breath as the man with the reins talked.

"Legend has it, these woods come alive at night with ghosts and goblins."

The little girls shrieked.

"But don't worry, we'll be back before they come out of the shadows." He turned back around, lifting the reins and snapping them once. The horses picked up on the command and began to walk.

Maddy snuggled deeper into John. "He scared me, and I'm an adult and fully aware there is no such thing as ghosts and goblins."

"These woods do have some spooky stuff happen. I've been out here at dusk and swore I heard and saw stuff. I'd hightail it back to the house."

"John Cooper, are you telling me you're afraid of the woods?"

He looked back over his shoulder. "Watch out!"

Five ghosts came out of the woods, waving their arms and making ghoulish sounds.

Maddy let out a blood-curdling scream, the kids in the wagon all cried out, the parents yelled, and a few even cursed. Then covering their mouths, quickly chuckled at their jumpiness at the fake ghosts.

Hitting John over and over with her balled hands, Maddy shouted, "You tricked me!"

He rolled his head back and laughed and laughed, roaring so loud he had tears in his eyes.

Maddy crossed her arms and huffed a loud breath.

Leaning over and winking, he kissed her arm. "Are you mad at me?"

"I'm mad at you, that's for sure." She hugged her crossed arms tighter.

"But you can't stay mad at me for long, right?" He nuzzled her neck.

"John," she said, pushing him back. "The children."

They both looked over to a row of staring faces. Just then, they all started clapping and making kissing sounds with their lips.

Maddy could feel her face grow warm and imagined her cheeks were as red as a tomato. John's face was turning a few shades of crimson as well, and if Maddy were a mind reader, she'd wager he was just as anxious to get out of the wagon as she.

Laughing and a bit embarrassed that children and parents alike caught them misbehaving, John grabbed Maddy by the hand and led her to the barn. Running like kids themselves, they fell into a mound of hay, the air whooshing out of their lungs as they hit the pile. Straw went flying, some landed in her hair, some in his.

"I'm having so much fun with you," she said, resting her head on his chest.

"And I with you." He plucked the straw from her hair and tossed it.

"It must be all this fresh air. I'm behaving like a teen." She touched her cheeks and felt the warmth.

"It must be having the same effect on me. I haven't

had this much fun or been this mischievous in a long time. If ever."

"I have a hard time believing that, John Cooper."

"Well, let's just keep it at a long time." He pulled her close, taking her by surprise.

"John, do you think we're maybe going a bit too fast?"

He released his hold.

"I mean, we've only known each other for a couple of months. We've shared some meals, had a few laughs together, even been through a terrifying ordeal when I found you almost unconscious. But I'm not sure all of that adds up to what we are doing now."

He fell backward on his arms, his elbows resting on the hay, and tilted his head. Peering at her through half-closed lids, his hair a bit tousled, he picked at the strands of straw, moving one to his mouth to chew on. She swallowed down the growing emotional pang she felt in her tightened throat, keenly aware of how handsome he looked, but also how cool and collected he'd seemed. Was he playing with her again?

"What is it that we're doing?" he asked.

"You know what I mean, John. This," she said, moving her hands between them.

"Kissing?" He leaned forward, still chewing on hay. "Getting closer? Learning about one another? I thought that's what people did when they were dating. But I've been out of the loop for a long time, so correct me if I'm wrong."

She jumped up and brushed her hand down her pant legs, removing the straw. "Dating?"

He stood. "Yes, dating."

"It's more like hanging out. People don't date. They hang out."

"Hang out. I see." He moved away, turning his back on her.

"John, this is what I mean. We come from different worlds. I'm the city girl with a self-esteem issue, and you're the country boy who...who..." She tossed her hands up in the air.

Moving toward her, he grabbed her hands and held them tight. "Who what? Finish your sentence."

"Who is a decent man, who deserves kindness and love. Something I can't give him." She pulled away from his hold.

He reached for her, but she pulled back more.

"Seriously? You don't feel capable enough to offer kindness and love? I don't believe that for a second."

"I thought maybe I could, but I'm broken." She hung her head.

"I'd like to break something of that Ryan's." He balled his one hand and punched the flat side of his other.

"It wouldn't help any. He's crushed my spirit, made me feel unworthy of true love. Damaged goods, I tell you."

"You're not damaged. Stop saying that. I could be damaged just as much. I'm sitting in a dark and lonely house night after night with my dead wife's dog, cooking and cleaning like some Amish woman, living like a hermit. That's damaged goods, Maddy." He groaned as he turned his back on her.

Now she'd done it. She'd messed up a perfectly good day. Shaking her head, she made her way toward the barn door. Just as she stepped one foot out, she stopped. Turning to face him, she parted her lips. Closing her mouth , she exited the barn. No words could fix it now. She'd blown any chance she'd ever have to develop a relationship with John.

Fluffy jumped up from his resting spot right outside the barn and ran up to Maddy. Maddy brushed the tears away that ran down her cheeks. Picking him up, she nuzzled him, feeling some security in the sweetness of their embrace.

Happy she didn't unpack the few belongings she'd brought, she put Fluffy in the seat and jumped right in after him. When they drove out of sight, the tears came down so hard and fast she had to pull over. Banging her head on the steering wheel, she wept hard and loud.

A tap on the window made her shoot straight up, wide-eyed with a racing pulse. She quickly wiped the tears away and stared at the face staring back at her. He opened the door and picking up Fluffy, slid in the passenger seat.

"What are you doing here?"

"I can't let you leave like this. What are we doing, Maddy?" His voice was subdued and shaky.

Shaking her head fervently, she grasped the steering wheel and focused ahead. If she dared to look in his eyes and see the hurt and pain she knew he was feeling because she was feeling it too, she didn't know what she'd say or do.

"Maddy. Look at me."

Testing her, that's what he was doing. She stayed focused, refusing to budge and look at him.

His hand rested on her arm, and bolts of electricity ran through her, making the hair on the back of her neck rise.

"Please, John. Just go."

"No. I'm not going. I care about you, darn it, Maddy. Why are you doing this to me?"

She gritted her teeth as tears rolled down her cheek.

"I know we can make this work if you'll just let me in," he pleaded.

She slowly turned, lifting her hand and wiping her

face. Her vision blurred from her puffy eyes, her lips and face burning from the streaming tears. She dropped her head back to try to clear the emotion. Resuming her focus on him, she blinked twice then spoke.

"John, I'm a mess. I want to stay, but I don't know how to handle all of this."

"I told you back at the farm we'd take it unhurriedly. You'll just take me a day at a time. I'll grow on you, I promise." He winked then smiled.

Turning the corners of her mouth up, Maddy reciprocated by flashing a weak smile back at him. She loved that he could find humor in all things.

"I don't de—"

"Don't say it, Maddy. You do deserve me. I deserve you too. When Sarah died in my arms that day, one of the last things she said to me was to make sure I found happiness again." His eyes filled with tears as he spoke about his beloved Sarah.

"I'm sure she did because that's the kind of woman she was. You know what Ryan told me?"

John shook his head.

"Don't let the door hit you, you know where."

John drew in a deep breath. "I'm not him. I'll never be him. He's despicable and arrogant, and if I ever see him, I'll show you how a man defends his woman's honor." He puffed out his chest to make his point.

"I'm your woman?" She inched closer toward him.

"I'd like that, but I'm not trying to rush you. We have plenty of time. Just come back with me. Let's get you settled into the loft, have some dinner, and just talk."

"Okay, John. I'm going to try my best to not run again. If I start to have a panicked look on my face, you'll know I'm thinking too hard again."

He leaned in. "I'll give you the space you need so you can work it all out in that pretty little head of yours. I don't want you to run again. I miss you when you're gone."

She shuffled inward. "I miss you too." She closed her eyes and moved closer, waiting for the touch of his lips on hers. And when the softness of his mouth melded with hers, she laced her arms around his neck and kissed him back.

Fluffy whined when he was getting squeezed out, making them both pull apart and snicker.

"Fluffy sure knows how to mess up a guy's kiss, doesn't he?"

Maddy brushed her hand down Fluffy's coat. "He likes you, but I know he's learning to trust again too."

Patting Fluffy on the head, John replied, "The farm is big enough for all of us and our insecurities. Let's work on them together."

He pulled open the door and hopped out. "Meet you back at the farm?" he asked.

"Yes, I'm going to whip a U-turn right here," she said, flashing him a wide grin.

"A U-turn, huh? That's a great euphemism for our relationship. We'll both make U-turns and learn to move forward."

"I love that idea," she said glowingly.

CHAPTER 15

"*L*et me help you with that," Maddy said, taking two logs from the huge pile he carried.

They both let them roll off their arms onto the ground with a thud.

"Tonight will be the most perfect night for a fire. Let me get it started." He picked up the kindling and criss-crossed it, plugging the holes with newspaper he'd wound tightly. He lit the ends of the paper, and when it ignited, he laid the first log on the flames. "Wine?" he asked, stepping back from the fire ring.

"Sounds good. Let me help."

He held the back-screen door open; she ducked under his arms and entered the back room that led to the kitchen. She went straight to the cupboard that held the wineglasses while he popped the cork. The *chugalug* of the wine as it poured was the only sound in the dimly lit room. He handed her a glass and clinked hers.

"To a new beginning," he said.

"To a new beginning," she echoed.

When they went back outside, the flames were dancing high. He tossed on another log and pulled up the Adirondack chairs, placing them near the pit.

She sat and immediately tilted her head back, looking up into the dark sky dotted with tiny white stars. "It's a gorgeous fall night. A little brisk in the air, a roaring fire, a glass of wine. It can't get better than this." She took a sip.

"I love this time of year. Especially after the brutal summer we've had," he said, gazing at the flames.

"Tell me what you and Sarah did for fun?" She twisted her body toward him and smiled.

"Well, let's see," he said, stumbling for words.

"If you don't want to talk about, just tell me to mind my own business," she said, giving him an out.

"We enjoyed taking long walks. We liked to cook and bake. But you probably already knew that."

"I know you learned your cooking skills from your mother. I should have known Sarah enjoyed it too."

"When you live on the land, you almost have to." He nodded.

"What else? What else did you do for fun?"

"I didn't think it would bother me this deeply to talk about our life together."

"If you'd rather not, I do understand, but it's hard for me to compete with someone I never knew who was so important to you. It's not the same with Ryan and me. He was a loser."

"This isn't a contest, Maddy. Ryan may have been a jerk, but he was important to you at one time. So, what drew you to him?" John asked.

She snuggled deep into the chair. Picking her legs up, she rested her heels on the ring of the firepit. "We met at a sports store."

"He was into sports? Hunting, fishing that sort of thing?" John asked.

Maddy shot him a warning stare. "Don't try to find some common thread with him."

"No, I wasn't. I was just curious what his sport was."

"Archery. He was into archery."

"I have an arch—" He quickly pressed his fingers to his lips and shook his head. "Sorry," he whispered.

"He came into the store and bought some arrows. I checked him out at the register. His card declined, and so he whipped out another to use. It declined as well. After three attempts, he got one to go through. The following week he came back for targets. I waited on him again. He remembered me, and we started talking about the credit card debacle."

"I remember the first time I saw Sarah. She'd come out to the farm to pick strawberries. Mom and Dad had a big patch back then, opened it up to folks to come pick their own berries. She'd tasted a few, too, and when she came up to the table to pay for her full baskets, and I mean they were rolling out full, I asked her if she was also going to pay for the ones she ate."

Maddy's jaw dropped wide open. "No, you didn't!"

"I sure did. She had berry juice all over her face and dripping down her arm. It was a dead giveaway she'd been sampling the goods."

Maddy laughed.

"I told her I was teasing, then her face turned bright red. The next time I ran into her was at the Amish market."

"She sounds like a quirky person. Just my kind of friend," Maddy said.

"She was always pulling pranks on me. One day I came home from plowing the fields. Nothing was cooking on the stovetop. I peered inside the oven. Empty. She was sitting in a chair over in the corner, crocheting. I asked her what was for supper, and she replied, 'make it yourself.'"

Maddy gasped. "That sounds like something I might say, but not your sweet Sarah."

"Right. Being the bigger person and not wanting to start a fight, I went into the kitchen and got out the pans and all the makings for grilled cheese sandwiches."

"I can't wait to hear how this ends."

John jumped up and set another log on the fire, then resumed his story, warming his hands by the fire. "I yelled out to her, asking if she'd also like one."

"She said, 'no, that's alright. It'll ruin my appetite.'"

Maddy leaned forward, her elbows resting on her legs. "You've got my total attention on this."

"I know I must have had a puzzled look on my face, and my tone probably was shaky at best. I asked her, appetite? Where are you going for dinner?"

"That's when she jumped up out of the chair, tosses her project to the table, and runs over to hug me. I'm standing there like I have egg on my face, trying to figure out what just happened."

"What did happen?" Maddy asked.

"It was the first of April." John grinned.

Maddy slapped her leg and fell back into her chair. "What did she do, yell April Fools?"

"Sort of like that. She led me outside, and on the picnic table was a spread fit for a king."

"She really was a jokester."

John jabbed the logs with a metal poker, sending up sparks. He sat back down. "Tell me something funny about Ryan."

"Back in the earlier days of our relationship, he was a decent guy. He changed gradually. That's why I stuck around so long. I didn't see it until it was there."

"I can see that happening," John said.

"But let me think. Oh, wait! I know. It was Christmastime, and he decided we'd go to the tree farm and cut our tree down. I was excited as my folks always had artificial trees. We dressed warmly, I made us a thermos of hot coffee and some snacks and off we went on this new adventure. We arrived at the tree farm and checked in at the shack. The guy tells us we're free to cut down any tree on his ten acres."

She stopped and took a sip of her wine before continuing. "Anyhoo, we start walking down the various paths and look at trees. Finally, we spot one that looks ideal. It's full, has a nice thing on the top for our angel and the perfect height. He starts sawing the tree, and just when it's almost cut, a field mouse runs up his leg!"

"Oh, this is going to be good," John said.

"He screams like a girl, drops the saw, and starts shaking his leg."

John let out a whoop.

"Right?" Maddy said, her gaze darting around his

face. "I help him by shaking his pant leg, and the critter scurries off."

"And the tree?" John's eyes crinkled at the corners, making Maddy's heart skip a beat.

"The tree. Oh yeah, the tree," she said, mesmerized by his handsome looks as the fire flickered. "He was so distraught over the ordeal, I had to finish cutting down the tree."

"I knew you had strong arms!"

"And I'm not afraid of a little old field mouse, either." She giggled.

"Should I put on another log, or are you tired?"

"I'm not tired. I could sit out here all night and talk."

"I have to get up early. Those cows will be angry if I don't milk their teats."

"Teats?"

"You do have a lot to learn about farming. Don't worry. I'll teach you everything you need to know."

"And cooking? Are you going to show me the way around a kitchen?" she teased.

He picked up her hand and held it. "I will teach you anything you want."

His hungry eyes made her limbs limp, and a small bead of sweat lay discreetly across her brows. It was the perfect moment for a kiss, but alas, it wasn't to be. A rustling sound startled them both.

Out of the shadows came the farm dogs, Hazel, Marcus, and Scruffy. They rubbed up against the arms of the chairs and with a *humph*, lay at John's and Maddy's feet.

"This is late for them to come in, isn't it?" she asked.

"Yeah, I usually go and round them up, but I was distracted." He winked at her, sending waves of excitement through her veins.

"I'm sorry."

"I'm just kidding, Maddy. I love this sort of distraction."

"Right. So, I think I'll turn in." She stood and stretched. "It's been a long and exhausting day."

He took the metal poker and separated the logs. Embers shot up in the air then fizzled away. A jug full of water sat nearby. He picked it up and doused the flames, squelching the fire to a pile of charred pieces of wood.

They let the big dogs into the house, gathered up Fluffy, and headed to the loft. It had been a perfect evening in her eyes, despite how it began with her emotional getaway and meltdown. She could be such a drama queen.

"I'm sorry about earlier," she started. "You know, when I behaved like a spoiled kid."

"You mean when you rushed out of here driving like

a maniac, pulling over to the side of the road and crying?" He looped his arm with hers as they walked.

"Yeah, that pretty much sums it up." She laid her hand on his arm and held it there.

"We all can have a bad day." He tugged her body closer.

"Bad day? You mean a psychotic episode?" She twisted her mouth.

"You've heard the expression, growing pains?"

"Of course," she said.

"That's what we are experiencing together. Growing pains."

They came to a halt at the barn door. "Thanks for saying that, John. I don't really know what came over me. I wanted to stay, but I just don't know if I fit in here."

John picked up her hands and laced their fingers. "I want you here. I think you fit perfectly fine. Sure, we've got some differences. You're a big city girl, and I'm just a country boy, but I know when I feel jittery inside and can't find the words because you're so darn pretty you jam everything up inside, and that my heart races like a horse during the Kentucky Derby. I think that means I sort of like you." He squeezed her hands.

Taking notice of her light-headedness, a shiver down her back brought her back to the moment. "You have a way with words, John," she said, her voice cracking with emotion.

"I've never been to college. All I have is a high school education. But I read. I read a lot."

"I figured you must because of the lack of electronic devices in your house." She smirked.

"It's just I go to bed early, I rise early, and then I fall back into bed at night exhausted. I just repeat my same routine. It's the farmer's life. But I did have a television once. I'd be willing to get another one."

"I don't want you to change for me, John. I have my ways to view shows. It's called my tablet."

"I had a nice time with you tonight. See you bright and early tomorrow." He leaned in and gave her a quick peck on the check.

She felt a bit disappointed with the brief smooch on the face. They'd already kissed. She wondered why he felt the need to dial it back a notch. She sighed.

"I'll have the coffee on early. See you." He turned and walked away.

"Hey, John," she called.

He turned on his heels while still taking steps backward. "Yep?"

"What time exactly is early?"

CHAPTER 16

Maddy left Fluffy in the loft with a promise of checking in on him later. As if he understood what she said, he curled up in a ball and blinked a few times, watching her finish dressing. In her desire to learn the ropes of farming, Maddy forgot she had nothing suitable to wear. Dressed in layers and jeans, she made her way toward the farmhouse. A soft yellow glow shone through the lacy curtains, and as she approached the porch, the aroma of freshly brewed coffee snaked around her, inviting her inside. She pulled open the screen and walked in. The hall that connected all the front rooms had a drafty feeling. Maybe he shouldn't leave his door open, she mused.

"Good morning, John."

He whirled around with two cups, one in each hand.

A wide smile bounced up quickly, followed by him holding out a cup. "Perfect timing."

She took the mug and lowered her nose, taking in the smell of coffee beans. "Thank you. I really needed this. Do you know it's four thirty in the morning? Even Fluffy couldn't figure out why I was getting up so darn early. By the way, I have to go let him out in a few hours." She drew the cup to her mouth and sipped.

John's gaze dropped to her feet and then back up to her eyes. "You need some farming duds."

"I know. But this will have to do for now."

He held up a finger. "Just a minute." He rushed out of sight, leaving her standing, drinking her coffee.

"These should fit you." He held out a pair of overalls and a pair of boots.

"Were these Sarah's?" she asked as she put her coffee down to further inspect the items.

"Yes. I hope you don't think it's weird that I'm offering them for you to wear."

Maddy shook her head. "Why are you keeping them?"

"I haven't been able to clean out her side of the closet or dresser."

Maddy reared her head back and paused.

"I've wanted to, but I don't know what to do with them."

"Maybe donate them to someone less fortunate?" Maddy shrugged.

"I had asked her mom if she wanted any of them when they were down here. She took a few sentimental things." He looked around the kitchen and located his cup. Holding the rim to his lips, he made a slurping sound as he drank.

"I can help you if you like. I'd like to buy my own clothes, though."

"It was weird, wasn't it." He placed his mug down and gathered the clothes and boots.

"Just a little. But it's okay. Growing pains."

PULLING a soft white cloth from a sealed container, he leaned forward on the stool, positioning himself near the cow's udder.

"It's very important we properly clean the udder before milking."

Maddy observed his every move. She didn't want to miss one single detail.

He tossed the used disposable wipe in the small empty bucket nearby. "Next, we dry it off."

He opened another container and removed a dry cloth, carefully wiping the udder.

"The last step before milking is lubricating."

Maddy's jaw dropped. "Lubricate the udder?"

"No, just the teat."

"And what do you use for that?" Maddy asked.

"Petroleum jelly works best." He began to rub the cow's teats with Vaseline.

"Now, pulling downward from the base of the teat and squeezing the milk, we'll fill this bucket."

The cow stood patiently while John milked it, only occasionally swaying and swatting its tail. The sound of the milk hitting the tin pail reminded Maddy of rain as it splattered on a tin roof. Thirty minutes later, he was finished. He cleaned off her udder once again and patted the cow on the hindquarter.

They had milked three cows when he asked her if she wanted to try. Being the team player she was, she took her place on the little stool, and following his directions, milked her first cow.

"This is hard work," she said after twenty minutes. "My arms are sore from holding them in this position."

John tipped his head toward the row of stalls. "We have ten more to do."

"With modern technology, isn't there some sort of mechanical milking machine?"

"Yes, but it costs money. It's on my dream list."

They moved to the next stall.

RESTING ON A BALE OF HAY, she devoured the bologna sandwich he'd made for her.

"Sorry lunch is nothing fancy," he said, taking a bite.

"A bologna sandwich never tasted so good." She took another bite, then swallowed it down with water.

"Thank you. Ezra makes the best sausages and bologna. You met him, remember?"

"Yes, the Amish fellow."

"His wife made the buttermilk bread too."

"Is the mayonnaise also homemade?"

"Yes. I buy very few packaged goods."

Maddy dropped her shoulders. "I don't think I'll ever measure up to these Amish folks."

"You don't have anything to prove, Maddy. We purchase from them what we don't make and grow. Simple as that. And for coffee, paper products, and some other things, we go to the local market." He winked.

"Thank goodness you said that. I was trying to figure out how in the world one would make toilet paper." She let out a small warble.

"That's a good one, Maddy. But just so you know, paper products come from trees."

"And you said you only have a high school education." She leaned in, bumping him.

When she moved back, he dropped his sandwich next to him and slipped his fingers under her hair. Pulling her in, he found her mouth, quickly kissing her without any resistance, sending her sandwich flying and her heart racing. A small groan escaped her lips, and before she could silence her desire for him, he deepened the kiss.

"I'm sorry," he said, putting distance between them. "I shouldn't have done that."

"I liked it, John. I liked it a lot." Her words came out smooth and sultry.

"When I was dating Sarah, I never looked at another girl. After we got married, I stayed true to her and never strayed. I've only been with one woman in that way."

"But kissing? You've kissed a few in your time, right?"

"Yes, a few. But they were always just kisses. I never felt the desire to go further."

Maddy's breath caught, making it difficult to speak. She prayed he didn't ask her any details about her sexual experience.

"You were so young when you and Sarah married. I couldn't even begin to put myself in your shoes."

"And I don't expect you to understand, nor do I want you to think I'm judging my experience with yours. We're each different. It's how we move forward together that is important." He picked up her hand and kissed her knuckles.

"What would the Amish community think about what we are doing?"

"I'm not Amish, remember?"

"I know. But humor me."

"During our courtship, Sarah and I kissed a lot. And we did a little more than that. That's how I knew she was the one. We waited until we were married before we consummated our love, but it wasn't for a lack of want or trying." He raised his brows and chuckled.

"I bet you think I'm a bad girl, having lived with Ryan."

He shook his head. "Not at all. I'm not a priest."

"I do admire your oath to wait, though."

"I didn't take any oath to wait. Sarah did. I just honored it."

"Now I feel dirty." She jumped up off the hay bale and brushed off her jeans, watching the straw scatter.

He jumped up and caught her hand as she began to move away. "Maddy, you shouldn't feel that way. That was a different time and a different situation. I'm not here to judge how you lived your life. I'm sure you didn't give yourself to Ryan without thinking it was true love."

She paused as she contemplated his statement. She did love him, but he wasn't her first, either. But how much should they divulge to one another? When is the past the past and how much sharing was she required to do?

"Let's just stop talking about it. We both have led way different lives. I'm attracted to you." She rolled her head back and grunted. "I'm so attracted to you," she said, making eye contact with him. "But I don't want you to ever feel I'm not good enough for you."

"I'd never think that." He pulled her close. "I told you, I'm not here to ridicule you, or tear your honor apart. It's two thousand and nineteen. I think what we do in private is our business. I'm glad to hear you're attracted to me. That you can't keep your hands off of me. That's good news." He slid his arms around her waist and jostled her around playfully, nipping at her mouth, trailing kisses down her neck, making her feel all squishy inside.

"John Cooper."

"Uh-huh," he said as he nibbled on her neck.

"The cows are watching."

CHAPTER 17

*L*ike most of their kisses, this one lasted only a few seconds. But Maddy wasn't mad about it.

His lips were so satisfying that even a few seconds on her mouth made her tingly inside.

After all the cows were milked, they headed to the hen house to gather eggs. He handed her a basket to collect them.

"This is easy. Way easier than milking," she said, inspecting the eggs as she set them carefully in her basket.

"I like to break up the tedious work with a little egg gathering," he said.

"Do you use all of these eggs?" Her gaze skated over the dozen eggs.

"I try to. They lay an egg about every other day.

Some of my hens drop one each day, though. If I have any extra, I always give to the women at the market."

Maddy held the basket with both hands, careful to not break the delicate eggs. John was so easygoing with her. She loved his caring direction as he taught her the ropes of farming. She had a lot to learn, though, and when he announced that next, they'd be out in the fields, she let him know she was up to the task.

"Remember, I'm a city girl," she said, tipping her head. "Be gentle."

"Haha, noted."

"I'll drop the eggs off at the house, you check on Fluffy, and I'll meet you at the back fields. I'll be the one in the driver's seat of the big green machine."

Maddy rushed to the loft to check on Fluffy. He was still sleeping. She rousted him up and took him outside. After he lifted his leg on various objects, she met John at the tractor. His gaze landed on the dog leash.

"You can't bring him up here. It's dangerous."

Her gaze dropped to Fluffy. "I can hold him on my lap."

"No, you can't. This is serious work, Maddy. Put him back inside with Sheba. Hurry up, though. The day is only so long."

She tugged at Fluffy's leash and led him to the farmhouse. She was a little perturbed with his tone with her. Where did the caring and soft-spoken John go?

She ran back to the tractor and jumped in. The seat vibrated under her as the engine rattled and shook.

"Sorry if I got a bit hot under the collar back there," he said as they moved slowly down the gravel road that paralleled the fields.

Looking away, she tried to will the tears away.

"There's been a few accidents out here with tractors. I didn't want Fluffy or you to be one."

"I understand," she said.

"I wouldn't want anything bad to happen to you or to your pup. That would be a sad day, indeed." He turned the tractor and drove through an opening that led to the fields.

"What are we going to do?" she asked, perking up some.

"We're going to cut the brush back that's near the woods. Down by the river."

"Why?"

"I need the trees to stay where they are and not grow onto my farming land. I grow crops and baby trees and other brush will pop up. Every couple of years, I do this during the late fall."

"I see."

He dropped the front-end loader and began to drive

along, digging up and scraping the earth, rolling over small saplings and offshoots from other trees and bushes. After about thirty minutes, he asked her if she'd like to try her hand at driving the machine.

They switched places, and Maddy, with the helpful direction of John, drove the tractor like she'd been driving that instead of her mobile grooming van for three years.

"You're doing great," he said, his encouraging words making her smile.

"This is fun," she said, raising her voice over the loud noise of clearing brush.

"You've earned yourself a badge today," he said.

She tried to concentrate on the job at hand, but she couldn't help but think about the sweet kiss they'd shared earlier, and how he made her feel. Could they really be a couple, she pondered.

"Go ahead and stop. Put the brake on like I showed you."

She did as he instructed. Instead of jumping out of the vehicle, she climbed over him while he moved over to the driver's side. But when they got close, she couldn't resist him. She dropped a kiss to his mouth then plopped down into the seat as he moved on over.

"What was that for?" He flashed her a grin.

"Just because. I mean, you were right there, and you

were hard to resist."

He dropped the gear, pulled up on the brake, and lifted the scoop. "We're done for the day."

"I'm exhausted. It's been a long day," she said.

They headed back to the barn, and he put the equipment away. She looked down at her tennis shoes, dusty and dirty, and with a small hole in the toe.

"I guess I need boots," she said, wiggling her big toe.

"Yep. There is a store in town that has everything you'll need."

"I'm going to hit the shower, then I'll come and get Fluffy. What's for dinner?"

He moved toward her and took her hands in his. "I like this new and confident Maddy."

Smiling wistfully, she swayed her body, swinging their hands. "I'm trying."

"Yes, you are," he said, stepping closer.

Parting her lips slightly, a desire to touch him led her to inch nearer. Separating their fingers, she brought her hand up to his face and traced the outline of his lips then brushed her hand to his cheek.

The pausing between them grew longer, and the emotion she felt grew stronger. Moistening her lips, she leaned in. "Kiss me."

Shaking his head slowly as if fighting off his own desire, his eyes grew dark and longing. He reached up and slipped his hand to her neck, and then urging her to come to him, he moved his mouth over hers, kissing her like she'd never been kissed before.

"That was nice." Her breathy words lingered.

Running his hands through his hair, he nodded. "Nice doesn't quite describe it enough for me."

He shot her another deep and longing look that told her if she didn't hightail it out of there, another kiss was coming.

"I better get cleaned up. I'll see you back at the house. Oh, wait. Fluffy." She placed her hands on her hips.

"Just leave him there. I'll feed him and Sheba. Come on over when you're ready."

MADDY LET the water rush over her head as she stood under the showerhead. Her mind told her it was too soon to feel these feelings for John Cooper, but her body told her otherwise. The aching that rocketed through her confused her and scared her at the same time. She'd not been new to love. Or maybe she'd never been in love. Only thought she was. She rinsed out the shampoo, finished showering, and got dressed. The loud hunger pangs coming from her stomach told her she'd earned her dinner. Every calorie.

"Something smells good," she said, entering the kitchen.

Fluffy ran up to her, wagging his tail.

"Tuna casserole. I hope you like it. I just threw it together." He looked up and smiled.

"I do."

"So, it's easy. I just take cooked egg noodles, a can of mushroom soup and a can of tuna and mix it all together. Add some shredded cheese, and top it with fried onion rings…also from a can, then pop it into the oven for twenty or thirty minutes just to bubbling."

"Wow, so you do know how to cook with processed foods."

"I do on long days like this one. But we'll have fresh green beans from the garden and crusty homemade soda bread."

"I'm so hungry I could eat brussels sprouts."

"You don't like brussels sprouts?" he asked.

She shook her head fervently.

"You haven't had them the way I make them, then."

"I don't like them period." She sat at the counter.

"Tomorrow, we'll go out and check on the fall crops. They're about done for the year. I will can some stuff, and then we'll plow over it and get ready for the next crop."

"It's never ending, is it?" She picked up a salt shaker

and stared at it.

"Farm life. It's hard. I told you it would be."

"Did Sarah help you with every aspect of it, or just now and then?"

"Now and then. She took care of the house, canned the vegetables, cooked and baked, took care of the animals. I did the plowing, planting, and mending fences." He slipped the casserole into the oven and joined her at the counter, pulling up a stool.

"I'm not much into cleaning and cooking. But I think we've already established that. I want to find something I'm good at. I love the idea of helping you around the farm, but I think my calling is different. I just can't put my finger on it." She slid back the stool. "Wine?" She moved to the cupboard and opened it.

"Aren't you making yourself comfortable in my house." He laughed. "Sure."

She grabbed two glasses and went to where the wine was stored. She did feel comfortable in his house.

"I'm betting you'll find something you love to do, Maddy. I know you were hoping the grooming business would take off, but it's just not that popular out here. In the bigger towns, yes, but out here in the country, grooming just isn't in demand."

"Right, and that's why I'm thinking about going in a different direction." She tasted her wine.

"You could open up a vegetable stand here on the property. Sell the crops, eggs, that sort of thing." He shrugged then drank his wine.

"With the Amish markets in town, would that even be a viable option?" She slid her finger around the rim of her glass.

"We're closer to the highway. We have tourists all the time driving by. They might like to stop at a stand. You could sell jars of honey too."

"You make honey too?" She knitted her brows.

He opened his mouth to speak. She held up her finger to silence him.

"I know. You live off the land."

He nodded, laughing. "That we do, Maddy Pryor."

When the timer rang, they let the dish cool for a bit, then they dug in. By then, Maddy was ravenous with hunger.

"Oh my. This is so good," she said, shoveling it in.

"Slow down. I don't want you to choke."

She dropped her fork and stared at him.

"What's wrong. Are you okay?" He leaned forward with a look of horror.

"I'm fine," she said, chewing her last bite. "I just had a lightbulb moment."

He settled back onto the stool and picked up his fork. "What's that?"

CHAPTER 18

John leaned back, rubbing his chin, keeping his gaze on her.

"You gave me the idea about tourists coming through here. Many people travel with their pets. I would be offering their furry babies a safe and comfortable resting place while they go sight-seeing or out to a restaurant. Some establishments are not very pet-friendly," she said.

"Right. You have a point. And so, you'd sort of be like a pet hotel." He tipped his chin.

"Yes! And, we could also sell jars of honey, and I make super cute dog bandannas. We could possibly have a small pet boutique. The problem will be, where do I find a place I can lease that would work for such an idea?" She crossed her arms, rapping her fingers on her skin.

John held up a finger. "I've got it. I know what we can do. I'll call in all the favors from the Amish community. They can raise a barn in a few days."

"A barn? I need power, water, and…"

"I know," he said, interrupting. "And the tool barn with the loft has all of that."

She narrowed her eyes. "I don't get it."

"I'll have a new barn made for the tractors and stuff. All I need is power. The existing tool barn has water and power because of the loft. We might need to insulate the walls better, but it's well built. It would be perfect for your pet hotel slash boutique."

"John, thank you so much, but I can't accept all of that. Maybe I can get a loan."

"Don't be silly. I've actually been thinking about building a new barn anyway to house my new equipment."

Maddy wrinkled her nose. "New equipment?"

"I've been seriously considering purchasing a seeder and another tractor."

"Oh. So, you aren't just doing this for me then?" Maddy eyed him suspiciously.

"Nope, not at all," he said, picking up his fork.

THE OLD BARN was transformed into the most beautiful pet hotel in over one hundred miles. Maddy knew this because she Googled it. The workers put their heart and soul into making it the best for her, and she couldn't thank them or John enough.

Standing back, she admired the sign hanging in front. "Ahh. That is so precious."

"Ezra's brother-in-law, the one who has the furniture and sign shop, he made it." John dipped his fingers in his pockets and shrugged.

"It's perfect. Maddy's Pet Stop."

"If you don't like it, we can change it, but the other night during dinner, you tossed that out as a possible name choice."

"I love it." She looped her arm through his, pulling his hand out of his pocket.

"Let's go inside." He took her hand.

"And this…so perfect. Love the double Dutch door." She beamed.

Inside, the smell of raw wood, stain, paint, and sawdust wafted up to her. Her gaze darted around the large space. Comfortable lounging places, a couple of dog runs for when the weather was bad, and in the back, a grooming room complete with a sink, table, and cabinets.

"John, this is perfect," she said, twirling around, looking at everything once more.

"It really turned out nicely. And look over here," he said, taking her by the hand.

"The boutique!" she yelled.

"These shelves are sturdy. They're not going anywhere. You can house the homemade honey here, and anything else we might sell, and then I thought over here you could put the pet products." He motioned toward the back wall where they had another couple of shelves along with a pegboard and hooks.

"That's a perfect place to put the bandannas and dog treats."

"Dog treats?" John asked.

"Yes. I did a search on Pinterest."

"Pinterest?" He furrowed his brows.

She shook off his naivety regarding Pinterest with a wave, then continued. "It's a site that shows how to make things. On the internet."

"I see. And what did you find out on this Pinterest thing on the internet," he said, slightly mocking her but with a smile.

"How to make homemade dog biscuits."

"And you're going to teach yourself how to make

them. The person who doesn't know her way around a kitchen," he said, the mockery still noticeable in his tone.

"I recall a certain someone telling me he'd teach me anything I wanted to know." She sauntered closer, her pouty mouth uncovered.

She dropped her gaze to his lips and then floated them back to his eyes.

"I did say that. So, it's a recipe then." He slipped his arms around her waist, slipping fingers in her belt loops, pulling her tight against him.

"Yes. I thought we could package them along with the bandannas I'll make. I actually found a company that already has them cut out. Easy peasy."

"On the internet," he said, tugging her hard against his body, making her tremble.

She nodded.

"You look so beautiful today. I don't know how I got so lucky to have you in my life, Maddy Pryor, but I'm glad you are." He dropped a sweet kiss to her mouth.

"I have to pinch myself at least once a day to see if I'm living this or dreaming," she said, hoping he'd kiss her again, longer.

"If this is a dream, don't ever wake me up." He regarded her steadily, his voice just above a husky whisper. He moved his warm lips across hers, gently parting them, his desire deepening the kiss. She groaned softly, letting him know he was pleasing her. He trailed kisses down her neck, reaching her earlobes. She clasped her hands around his neck and kissed him with all she had. She'd make sure he knew this wasn't any dream.

Fraught with emotion, they stepped back, taking a moment to catch their breath. He rubbed his jawline thoughtfully while she marveled at the breadth of his shoulders, his dazzling blue eyes, and the entire package that made up John Cooper.

She crossed her arms beneath her breasts, wondering how she got to this place, and was it for real, and more importantly, was it forever. She'd never know the answer to that for certain. Maybe over time. But there was still a part of her unaccepting of this sweet love that John Cooper was so gently handing to her, and did he really care for her or just trying to fill a void?

"John, before we move forward, I have something to ask you. It could just blow up in my face, and I'll be tearing down the road again. But I have to know. Are you on the rebound?"

"I could ask you the same thing, Maddy. But I choose to believe you're here for a reason that's bigger than the two of us." He stepped back into her space.

She lowered her gaze.

Tipping her chin up with a finger, he locked gazes with her. "Right? I mean, I could assume the same of you. Ryan hurt you, I was here. But I don't think that's how this all plays out. I think. I believe," he emphasized, "we were brought together for a reason. You can call it rebound, but I want to call it living. Sarah wanted me to be happy and live my life to the fullest."

"But Ryan didn't want that for me. He couldn't care less about my happiness."

"That's right. But it's within you. It's within both of us to find our happy place. I can't shuffle along in that house sad and blue any longer. And you, you are too beautiful and kind to not have love in your life." He rocked her in his arms. "I care about you so much. And I'm not pushing you to do anything you're not ready to do."

"For a country boy, you're pretty profound," she said teasingly.

"We learn a lot about life and death out here. It will either make you strong or weak as a newborn baby. I chose to be strong. And I think you are too."

Wrinkling her nose, she raised her chin and smiled. "I do deserve to be happy, and I deserve you."

A sexy smile crossed his mouth, making her want to smash her lips against his. A sexy smile he wouldn't have even known he could do. Swallowing down the lump in her throat, she wished away the tears that tried to also make an appearance. No time for tears, Maddy Pryor, she said to herself.

The deep, longing look he gave her made her rethink. Maybe he did know he was downright sexy. And when he swooped her up into his strong arms, making his way toward the stairs to the loft, she melted into him, wrapping her arms around his neck, and believing finally, she deserved his love.

EPILOGUE

Maddy's Pet Stop took off like a bullet. Travelers from near and far stopped in to let their fur babies stay awhile, get a bath and some tummy rubs while they waited for their owners. Fluffy offered great moral support to all the shaking little dogs only to win them over and make them feel right at home.

John and Maddy teamed up in the kitchen to bake the dog biscuits. They were such a hit; she had a hard time keeping them on the shelves.

They added things to the boutique like honey, jam and preserves, and John's famous elderberry syrup. And when they had extra eggs, they sold them, as well as glass jugs of fresh milk.

Maddy still called the loft home, but she spent so

many hours over at the farmhouse, it was like a second home. They'd kept up this routine with their relationship for almost a year when she got the surprise of her life.

Dropping down to one knee, he took her hand in his. "We've been in this relationship for almost a year now. I can't imagine spending my life without you."

"John, you don't—"

He held up a hand and hushed her. "Let me finish, please."

She nodded.

"I love you with all of my heart. You make me want to get up each day and see the good in life. I know you're happy too. You smile all day and night, you sing and hum tunes, you're not on the internet that much anymore. You love to spend time just with me."

"I do, John. I love living out here on the land, working with my hands, working alongside you. I'm happy to be doing what I want with the Pet Stop, but mostly, I'm just happy."

"Will you marry me?"

"Yes. I'll marry you. But under one condition."

He tilted his head. "I'm listening."

"I know you're a country farmer, and I'm from the big city. And we women from the city like to do things our way. We're independent, don't want to be told what to do or say."

"I'd never take your individuality away, Maddy. That's who you are. I love you for you."

"Well, I'm here to tell you that I'm okay with you cooking. I can give up that part of my independence. I've enjoyed you making all those delicious meals. I'm good at washing dishes, and you're great at cooking. I'm good with reversing the roles."

He pulled her up and dropped a big kiss on her mouth. "Maddy, Maddy, Maddy. I love you so much." He wrapped his arms around her and hugged her tight.

"I love you too," she whispered, a small smile crossing her mouth as he swayed her in his arms.

ABOUT THE AUTHOR

A USA Today bestselling author, Debbie writes sweet contemporary romance and women's fiction. She lives in South Carolina with her husband and two dachshund rescues, Dash and Briar. Debbie loves to hike, work in the garden, and on most sunny days, you can find her enjoying her backyard. She's an avid supporter of animal rescue, and as such, pledges to happily donate a percentage of all book sales to local and national rescue organizations. When you purchase any of her books, you're also helping animals.

To find out more about Debbie, check out her website at

www.authordebbiewhite.com

and Facebook at Debbiewhitebooks

ALSO BY DEBBIE WHITE

Romance Across State Lines

Texas Twosome

Kansas Kissed

California Crush

Oregon Obsession

Florida Fling

Montana Miracle

Pennsylvania Passion

Romantic Destinations

Finding Mrs. Right

Holding on to Mrs. Right

Cherishing Mrs. Right

Charleston Harbor Novels

Sweet Indulgence

Sweet Magnolia

Sweet Carolina

Sweet Remembrance

Others

Perfect Pitch

Ties That Bind

Passport To Happiness

The Missing ingredient

The Salty Dog

The Pet palace

Billionaire Auction

Billionaire's Dilemma

Coaching the Sub

Christmas Romance – Short Stories

www.ingramcontent.com/pod-product-compliance
Lightning Source LLC
Chambersburg PA
CBHW070955190726
48292CB00004B/1460